Thank you
taking the
my Booktrib Book Giveaway!
Very much appreciated! If
you like my book, I would

FOREVER HONOR

appreciate it if you would
leave a review on Booktrib,
Amazon, Goodreads, or Xlibris.
Or post a picture of it on
Social Media (Facebook,
Twitter, etc). Enjoy!

Sincerely,

Andrew L Smith

FOREVER HONOR

ANDREW L SMITH

Library of Congress Control Number: 2022922504
ISBN: Hardcover   978-1-6698-5847-8
             Softcover   978-1-6698-5846-1
             eBook   978-1-6698-5845-4

Print information available on the last page.

Rev. date: 12/02/2022

To order additional copies of this book, contact:
Xlibris
844-714-8691
www.Xlibris.com
Orders@Xlibris.com
848670

Contents

CHAPTER ONE

The Unknown

It's a Friday morning in Center City, Illinois and Lucas Lightfoot is lying in bed with his wife Shelia Lightfoot whom is still sleeping soundly. He opens his eyes heavenward and he can hear the angry wind whipping on this brutally cold January morning. It snowed a couple of inches the previous day and Lucas is dreading having to face the weather elements. But, as a Warehouse Supervisor at Martha's Cheese Factory, he has to be there and he's always aware that he needs to be a good role model for his employees. Lucas glances over at his alarm clock and becomes startled when he realizes that it stopped a couple of hours earlier. Lucas fears that he might be late for work and he reaches over to the small table next to their bed and picks up the television remote. He turns on the television and scans various channels and finally settles on Fox Twenty-Three Morning News. He looks toward the lower right portion of the screen and the current time reads ten minutes after six o' clock. Lucas realizes that if he doesn't hurry up that he might be late for work and he gets up out of bed softly because he doesn't want to wake up Shelia. He makes his way toward the bathroom and short time later; he enters the bathroom and closes the door behind him and begins to freshen up. He's thankful that he routinely sorts out his work clothes the night before, because it saves him time, just like Shelia suggested.

After Lucas finishes, he studies his appearance in the mirror and he's not pleased with his hair. He combs it again and is now satisfied with it and on his way back to their bedroom, Lucas glances up at the antique clock, and the time reads six-thirty a.m. He shakes his head in disgust and when Lucas re-enters their bedroom, Shelia is still sleeping soundly. Lucas considers fixing himself a quick breakfast, but decides against it and he tells himself that he'll pick up some breakfast at Mc Donald's. He opens their closet door and takes a heavy, hooded coat off a hanger and then grabs a Chicago Bears' winter cap off the shelf above. Lucas places the items on the edge of their bed and then walks over to a drawer and takes out a couple of pairs of black socks. He sits on the bed and puts his socks on and then Lucas puts on his high-top Nike tennis shoes. He remembers that his winter gloves are already in his coat pocket and he proceeds to put on his coat, hat, and gloves. After he puts on the items, he tries to remember if he needs anything else before leaving for work and he realizes that he needs his car keys. He picks them up off a nightstand and before Lucas leaves the house, he looks over at Shelia. He walks over to her and leans over and gently kisses her on the forehead. She feels his lips and mumbles for Lucas to have a great work day and he wishes her the same. He leaves the bedroom and heads toward the front door and on his way out, he hears their two teenage sons, Chester and Melvin Lightfoot snoring in a deep sleep. They're both students at Center City High School and Chester is a senior and Melvin is a sophomore. Lucas closes the door and walks toward his car and the wind is whipping furiously. For a brief moment, he thinks that it might knock him down and snow is scattering in various directions. Branches of trees are shaking, and some people are running on the sidewalk. Lucas gets into his car and warms his engine for several minutes before driving off to Mc Donald's. Ten minutes later, he pulls into the Mc Donald's Drive Thru and he orders a number three breakfast combo. He drives off and a short time later; he pulls into Martha's Cheese Factory parking lot. His facial expression changes into confusion when he sees employees mulling around the building and not inside. Lucas parks his car near the company entrance and before he gets out of the car, he glances down at his watch. It is seven o' clock and Lucas gets out of the car and observes some employees staying warm in their vehicles. Other employees approach Lucas and are obviously unhappy. His long-time employees Jacob Wright and Evelyn Hampton voice their displeasure to Lucas.

"Lucas, what the hell is going on?! The company posted a sign on the entrance door that says that the plant is closed indefinitely!", Jacob said, fuming.

"Are we going to work today Lucas? Why would the company do something like this to us Lucas? It's cold as hell out here", Evelyn said, taking a sip of her Starbucks Coffee.

"Everybody calm down and relax. I don't know what's going on, but I'm going to find out", Lucas assured them.

"Lucas, the temperature is in the teens and with the wind chill, it's probably close to zero", she said, slightly shivering.

"It is brutally cold and I suggest that y' all warm up inside your vehicles. When I find out what's going on, I'll let everyone know."

"Okay", Jacob said.

The employees get into their vehicles and wait for further information. Lucas gets into his car and he pulls out his company cell phone and dials the number of the Plant Supervisor, Moose Davidson. The phone rings three times and on the fourth ring, Moose answers it.

"Hello", Moose said.

"Hello Moose. This is Lucas Lightfoot and I wanted to know if you can tell me why the company is closed right now. I have some disgruntled employees that are ready to work and it's freezing out here", Lucas said.

"I know that this is a terrible situation and I feel sympathetic for everyone", Moose said.

"We can't work and what am I supposed to tell our employees?"

"Lucas, this situation is out of my control."

"What do you mean? And why didn't we receive a proper notice about what was going to happen?", Lucas demanded.

"Lucas, our company lost a major account and it severely reduced our need for production", Moose said, grimly.

"Well, I know that production has been slower than usual. But I never imagined that things would become this bad."

"Our company has also filed for bankruptcy. We've been hanging on by a thread financially for the last couple of years. Our corporate executives told me that the company is going to sell as many assets as possible."

"Martha's is going out of business?", Lucas asked, shocked.

"I'm afraid so and I feel terrible for our employees. Many of them have devoted so many years of their lives to our company. Some of them came to work for us right out of high school and have been employed here for ten, fifteen years, and longer", Moose said, shaking his head.

"So do I and I'll be praying for their families. Well, at least everyone can collect Unemployment Insurance."

"I admire your attitude Lucas. I want you to know that I appreciate your efforts and service to our company. You're a good man Lucas and I wish you and your family well."

"Thank you for the kind words Moose and it was a pleasure working with you. My wife Shelia and I have two teenage sons and I dread having to tell them news like this."

"I wish that I had better news for you Lucas."

"I know. Well Moose, I'm going to notify our employees about what's happening."

"I need to tell you one more thing Lucas."

"What is it?"

"The employees need to clean out their lockers and gather their belongings. I'll be up there within the next ten to fifteen minutes along with some Sheriff's Deputies."

"Are you kidding me Moose? We're unemployed now and you're going to bring Law Enforcement up here? What kind of a stunt is this?"

"I understand how you feel Lucas, but our corporate people gave me a direct order. My hands are tied."

"This is wrong damnit and we're not criminals! We don't deserve this and it's humiliating!" Lucas said, fuming.

"The corporate people are afraid that the employees might become violent. They're afraid that they might damage the building and they want to make sure that the employees gather their belongings. We want them to peacefully exit the building without incident", Moose said.

"I think that we know how to conduct ourselves like adults", Lucas said, sarcastically.

"We'll be up there shortly and good-bye Lucas."

"Good-bye Moose."

Lucas hangs up disgustedly and then lets out a long sigh of dread. He composes himself and then gets out of his car and motions for the employees to gather around him. They all make their way to where he's standing and when everyone is surrounding Lucas, he breaks the news to them.

"I'm sorry to inform everyone that none of us are employed at Martha's anymore. Our plant supervisor, Moose Davidson just informed me that our company is going out of business. He wants us to clean out our lockers and then exit the building", Lucas said.

"How are we supposed to get our stuff when we can't get in?", Jacob asked, angrily.

"Moose will be here in ten to fifteen minutes to let us in. And so that you won't be caught off guard, he's going to bring some Sheriff's Deputies with him."

"They don't have to treat us like that!"

"This sucks!", Evelyn said.

"I know and I suggest that y' all get back into your vehicles and sit tight until they arrive."

"Okay."

Lucas and his employees get back into their vehicles and wait for them to arrive. While he's waiting, Lucas begins eating his Mc Donald's breakfast and in between bites, he scans his radio and listens to various musical artists. Fifteen minutes later, Lucas sees a black SUV and a couple of sheriff cars pulling into the company parking lot. Eventually, the vehicles park near the company entrance and Moose and the sheriff's deputies get out of their vehicles. A short time later, Lucas gets out of his car and approaches Moose and the deputies while motioning for the employees to join them at the entrance. When Lucas and the employees are gathered around Moose and the deputies, Moose speaks to them.

"Hello everyone, I'm Moose Davidson and I'm sorry that we had to meet under these circumstances", Moose said.

"Sorry isn't going to feed my family", Jacob blurted out angrily.

"Our company will do everything that we can to help y' all secure new employment. We will give y' all good references and referrals. In the meantime, everyone can collect Unemployment Insurance."

"This is cold-blooded and a slap in the face to all of us."

"I wish that things would've turned out different for everyone, but unfortunately, there's nothing that I can do about it", Moose said.

"This is bullshit!", Evelyn said.

"Our corporate executives told me that they want everyone to clean out your lockers and remove any food or beverages that you might have in the company refrigerator. The deputies will be monitoring everyone as you are removing your items and they will make sure that the company parking lot is secure. And when we're satisfied that everything is in order, then we'll lock the entrance door. After that, everyone will be ordered to leave the premises. Does anyone have any questions?", Moose asked, looking around.

No one has any and Moose unlocks the entrance door and the employees enter the building following Moose and Lucas. The sheriff's deputies walking alongside of them and as the employees are walking toward their lockers, some of them are mumbling obscenities. Others are crying and consoling each other and some employees are shocked and can't hide their disappointment no matter how hard they try. As Lucas is cleaning out his office, he has a somber expression on his face and the reality of being unemployed is starting to hit him. He's thinking about all the years that he worked at Martha's and the sacrifices that he made for the company. He reflects back to all the weekends that he worked and being away from his family all those years. He trained and mentored numerous employees and completed company educational courses in an effort to move up the company ladder. He went to work not feeling well when he probably should've stayed home and let Shelia nurse him back to health. Now Lucas feels that his efforts were for nothing and feelings of depression are starting to kick in. He is anxious and fearful of what the new chapter of his life might bring for him and his family. Lucas wonders if he'll be able to get another supervisor's position and as a black man, he knows that it's not going to be easy. Lucas tries to snap out of his depressing thoughts and focus on some positive things about his situation. Shelia has her full-time job at the Allen Cardboard Company so he doesn't have to be in a big rush to get another job immediately. Chester and Melvin are teenagers and not young children, and they're both doing well in school. He can use this idle time to spend more time with his family, especially on weekends, and monitor the house. These thoughts uplift his spirits a little bit and thirty minutes later, he finishes cleaning out his office. Lucas walks around the plant to check on the progress of the employees and most of them have cleaned out their lockers and only a few remain. A short time later, they finish and indicate to Lucas that they're finished and Lucas nods his head approvingly and the employees leave the building. Lucas looks around and sees Moose and the Sheriff's Deputies nearby and tells them that all the employees are finished and have left the plant. They exit the building, and Moose locks the entrance door and Moose asks Lucas to turn in his office key and he hands them over to Moose. They shake hands and exchange good-byes and the Sheriff's Deputies order everyone to leave the company premises. The employees make their way to their vehicles and they all gradually leave and Lucas is one of the last employees to leave. Before he leaves, Lucas sits in his car for about five minutes and stares blankly at the "Martha's Cheese Factory" sign for the last time. Tears start rolling down his cheeks and he reaches over into his glove compartment and pulls out some Kleenex and dries his face. When he's finished, he dumps the Kleenex into his ashtray and then starts up his engine and lets his car warm up for about ten minutes. When he's satisfied with the warmth of his car, Lucas drives home. When he arrives home, he walks in and Shelia is shocked and asks why he's home so early.

"I lost my job and our company is permanently closed", Lucas said, dejected.

"What? Why did they go out of business and why are they now just telling y' all?", Shelia asked, angrily.

"Martha's had severe financial problems and the need for production was drastically reduced. This is one hell of a way of beginning a new year", Lucas said, shaking his head.

"Lucas, you were loyal and dedicated to that company for twenty years. You deserved much better than this", Shelia said.

"There's nothing that I can do about it now. What's done is done."

"Lucas, I'll fix you something to eat and what do you want?"

"Do we have some ham left?"

"Yes we do."

"Shelia, a ham and cheese sandwich and a cup of coffee would be nice."

"You've got it sweetie. You're in luck with the coffee because I just made some and the pot just finished brewing. Anything else Lucas?"

"That's all sweet heart and thank you. The food and coffee will go a long way toward calming my nerves", Lucas said, gently massaging his temples.

"Okay. Sit down, relax, and kick off your shoes and check out what's on television if you want to", Shelia encouraged him.

"I love and appreciate you Shelia", Lucas said, winking at her.

"Right back at you Lucas", Shelia said, winking back at him.

"Shelia, I almost forgot to ask you about the boys. Did they make it off to school okay? Was everything normal around here?"

"They're fine and it was a typical school day."

"Good."

"I'll get your sandwich and coffee."

"Okay."

Shelia walks into the kitchen and fixes the sandwich and pours up the coffee in a white, foam cup. She then puts three tablespoons of sugar and one tablespoon creamer into the coffee and stirs it up. Before she goes back into the living room, Shelia sees a couple of small bags of Jalapeno Cheetos laying on the kitchen cabinet. She decides to ask Lucas if he wants a bag and he says yes and Shelia puts it on a plate, along with some napkins. She takes the items to Lucas and when she goes back into the living room, Lucas graciously accepts the food and coffee. He thanks her while placing the items on the living room table and Shelia sits alongside Lucas while he consumes a couple of bites. They silently watch television and are watching Judge Faith Jenkins. Shelia doesn't like the vibe that she's feeling from Lucas and she strikes up a conversation.

"Lucas, what's going through your mind? You can talk to me", Shelia said, concerned.

"Shelia, I don't know how I'm going to break the news to our sons. Chester will be graduating from high school this year and Melvin is only a couple of years behind him. I want both of them to attend college and we know that Melvin really has his heart set on college", Lucas said.

"Me too Lucas and I have no doubt that they will. Chester has a good chance of earning a College Basketball scholarship and Melvin is the captain of his debate team. They both have coaches and teachers that might be able to pull some strings for them."

"You're right about that."

"Our family is going to be fine and we just have to trust and believe in God."

"And I'm worried about us being able to keep up with our mortgage payments. What if I'm unemployed for a long period of time? How would we make it Shelia? We've worked so hard to give our children the best life possible."

"Stop worrying Lucas because we're going to be okay."

"I'm forty-five years old and I don't know if I'll ever get another Supervisor's position. Black men don't get positions like that every day and I might have to go back to being a regular employee", Lucas said.

"I know that it's difficult right now Lucas, but you need to try and think positive. We're going to get through this", Shelia said, gently patting him on the shoulder.

"I gave my heart and soul to that company and what do I have to show for it? A pink slip and becoming a member of the unemployed" Lucas said, bitterly.

"Lucas, you did your best and the only thing that we can do now is plan for the future. And the Unemployment money that will be coming in will be better than nothing", Shelia said.

"I'm going to file my Unemployment Claim on Monday Morning."

"Lucas, this could be a blessing in disguise and you could receive a better job. When one door closes, another one opens."

"Well, that's a unique way of looking at this situation."

Lucas and Shelia enjoy each other's company until the early afternoon. Shelia has to get ready for her second shift job at the Allen Cardboard Company. After she leaves for work, Lucas decides to cook for his family and he cooks a variety of foods that have his taste buds jumping for joy. He fixes pork chops, his favorite meat, homemade macaroni and cheese with green bell peppers, sprinkled with corn flakes on top, and a couple of large cans of green string beans. He doesn't have to concern himself with something for everyone to drink because there are a couple of two-liters of Pepsi and Mountain Dew in the refrigerator. When he's finished cooking, Lucas feels a sense of pride and loves the beautiful smell of the kitchen. He sniffs the air several times and then flexes his muscles. Later that evening, Lucas is sitting at the kitchen table with Chester and Melvin and he asks them how their school day went.

"Well Dad, we had a rough basketball practice today. Coach Jenkins had us run a lot of laps and he chewed us out throughout practice. He wasn't happy with our defense against Lincoln Central and he made that loud and clear", Chester said.

"Your coach was using tough love and I'm sure that y' all will play much better the next game. By the way Chester, what team do y' all play against next?", Lucas asked.

"We play Johnson Academy at home tomorrow night at seven o' clock."

"Do you need a ride to the game?"

"That would be nice."

"Well, I can take you to and from the game."

"Okay."

"Melvin, how was your day?", Lucas asked, looking in his direction.

"It was alright. Coach Hamilton has been emphasizing the importance of concentration and being able to articulate our ideas more clearly. Our first debate competition is against Norwood Lutheran next week and Coach wants to make sure that we're prepared", Melvin said.

"What are some of the things that y' all debate about?"

"A variety of subjects because Coach Hamilton wants us to be well-rounded debaters. One day, we might debate a Supreme Court Case, or during another one, we might debate the best solutions to solve a problem. Coach always keeps us on our toes."

"He sounds like a good coach."

"He is. Coach Hamilton tells us that debating skills can help improve our public speaking skills and develop good job interview skills. Did y' all know that public speaking is the number one fear of people in the United States?", Melvin asked.

"I didn't know that and I would've guessed that it would be a fear of heights."

"And I would've guessed that it would be a fear of spiders", Chester said.

"Those are both good answers, but public speaking is number one."

"You learn something new every day", Lucas remarked.

"Coach Jenkins told me that his alma mater, Chicago State University has shown interest in me playing College Basketball for them", Chester said.

"That's great Chester", Lucas said.

"And he also told me that Bradley University and the University of Northern Iowa have also showed interest in me."

"Chester, keep up your grades and stay out of trouble. Keep on doing what you've been doing."

"I will."

"Dad and Chester, Coach Hamilton believes that I might be able to get at least a partial scholarship to some Universities, especially if I continue to perform well in my debates", Melvin said.

"Stick with debating Melvin because it could open the doors of College for you. I would also encourage you to talk to your Guidance Counselors and Teachers because they can give you some valuable information", Lucas said.

"I'll keep that in mind Dad."

"Dad, we didn't even ask you how your day was. Did you have a good day?", Chester asked.

"It wasn't a good one boys and your father will be around the house for some time", Lucas said.

"What do you mean Dad? I don't understand."

"Neither do I", Melvin said.

"Our company permanently closed today and I'm unemployed."

"They let you go? That's bogus!"

"That's life boys and no one ever said that it was fair. All you can do is give your best effort", Lucas said.

"Dad, does that mean that going to College is out of the question?", Melvin asked, concerned.

"Melvin, don't fix your mouth to ask that question and you're both still going to College. That's not going to change and your mother and I want both of you to have careers. I want y' all to have a better life than your old man. In today's world, especially as young black men, you need a good education."

"Dad, I don't want to be a financial burden on you and Mom. I can---

"Melvin, did you hear what I said? I don't want to hear another word about this. Your mother and I just want y' all to keep your grades up and stay out of trouble. We want both of you to stay on the success road and we'll take care of everything else", Lucas assured them.

"Okay", Melvin said.

Lucas and the boys continue conversating and when they're finished eating, they all pick up their eating utensils and plates and wash them and put them into their proper places. Chester and Melvin then retire into their rooms and begin doing their homework while Lucas relaxes and watches television. Nothing special happens the rest of the day and two days later, Lucas and the family are preparing to attend church at Zion Missionary Baptist Church, which is their church home. An hour before church service is scheduled to start, Chester walks into the living room and tells Lucas that he's not feeling well.

"Dad, my stomach feels terrible", Chester said, clutching his stomach.

"Is it hurting?", Lucas asked.

"No, it just feels funny."

"How?'

"Maybe I ate something that didn't agree with my stomach or maybe I have an upset stomach", Chester said, moaning.

"We have plenty of time before church starts. I want you to go into the bathroom and take some Pepto Bismal and that should calm your stomach down", Lucas said.

"I don't know if that will help Dad. Oh man", Chester said, rubbing his stomach.

"Chester, forget about trying to get out of attending church because you're going", Lucas said, firmly.

"Come on Dad, do I have to go? The sermons are so long that I sometimes find myself falling asleep."

"Everyone in our family is going and what makes you think that you shouldn't have to go? Just because you scored thirty-five points last night doesn't mean that you're going to weasel out of church. Our family needs to give God more of our time, so get over your inconvenience."

"Okay Dad", Chester said, not pleased.

"I'm proud of you Chester and you really came through for Center City in the fourth quarter. And the best part is that Center City won", Lucas said, smiling and giving Chester two thumbs up.

"Thank you Dad."

"You're welcome and Melvin doesn't get any special privileges either. Just because he's the captain of his debate team doesn't mean that he can get out of attending church either. And your mother and I expect both of you to do your chores around the house."

"I get the message Dad."

"Good. Now finish getting ready and don't forget to straighten your tie."

"Okay."

Chester walks toward the bathroom and finishes grooming himself and moments later, Shelia comes out of their bedroom and Lucas' jaw drops with delight and his eyes blink more than usual. He is pleasantly surprised at her stunning appearance and Shelia's hair is shoulder length, her face is glamorous, and her face is glowing. Her skin is flawless and Shelia is sporting a dynamic black dress and stockings and wearing sparkling earrings and red, high-heeled shoes. At that moment, Lucas believes that she's the most beautiful woman in the world and Shelia sees the star-struck look on Lucas' face. She blushes and then asks Lucas if he approves of her appearance. He nods his head up and down and then he begins talking to her.

"Shelia, you look like a supermodel! Wow!", Lucas said.

"Thank you Lucas, but I think that you might be getting a little carried away", Shelia said, blushing again.

"I don't think so and you look great!"

"Well, I'm happy that you love my look Lucas. By the way, you look so handsome wearing your blue suit, white tie, and your face is so well-groomed."

"Thank you Shelia and I was having second thoughts about wearing this suit."

"I don't know why you would because that suit looks perfect on you. Besides, you know that blue is my favorite color", Shelia reminded him.

"I forgot about that", Lucas said, breaking out into a huge smile.

"Where are the boys? Are they almost ready?", Shelia asked.

"Well Chester is in the bathroom freshening up and I don't know how far along Melvin is. Let me call him. Melvin, are you ready for church?! How far along are you?!", Lucas asked.

"I'm almost ready and I just have to wash my face, comb my hair, and brush my teeth", Melvin said.

"Okay, Chester is in the bathroom right now and I don't think that he'll be in there much longer. Let me check."

"Okay Dad."

As Lucas is about to check on Chester's progress, he re-enters the living room and indicates to Lucas and Shelia that he's prepared for church. Lucas yells out to Melvin that he can now use the bathroom and Melvin comes out of his room and goes to the bathroom to finish grooming. Ten minutes later, Melvin joins the rest of the family in the living room and Lucas and Shelia investigate their appearance and voice their approval. Before they leave, Lucas asks if anyone has to use the bathroom before they leave and everyone tells him no and then they all walk out. Fifteen minutes later, they arrive at Zion Missionary Baptist Church and Lucas parks his car in the church parking lot. The family gets out and are heading toward the church entrance and when they're almost there, a man's voice yells at them.

"Lucas and Shelia! Lucas and Shelia!", he yelled.

Lucas and Shelia look around in search of the mysterious voice. Moments later, long time church members Wilbur Baxley and his wife Mary Baxley approach them. They all break out into big smiles and embrace each other and their faces are glowing at the unexpected encounter. They stare at each other briefly and then Wilbur strikes up a conversation.

"Lucas and Shelia, how have y' all been? It's been some time since we've seen y' all", Wilbur said.

"I know and our family has been fine. Is everything okay with y' all?", Lucas asked.

"Everything is good and our children are grown and they're doing well", Wilbur said, proudly.

"That's a blessing and both of you should pat yourselves on the back", Shelia said.

"It is and we're thankful. How old are Chester and Melvin now?"

"Chester is seventeen and Melvin is fifteen."

"It only seems like yesterday that you boys were children and now you're developing into young men. Wow!", Mary said.

"Chester, I read the sports profile article they had on you in the Center City Press Gazette. You're quite a basketball player and leading your conference in scoring is quite an accomplishment", Wilbur said.

"Thank you, Mr. Baxley."

"You're welcome and keep on striving to be the best that you can be."

"Scoring all those points is nice, but I want to help our team win. After all, basketball is a team sport."

"I admire that attitude."

"Melvin, are you on any sports teams?', Mary asked.

"No, but I played on the freshman football team last year, but I didn't like it. I tried out for our debate team and I fell in love with it and I'm the captain", Melvin said.

"It's a great thing when you discover something that you enjoy."

"You're the captain, so your coach obviously sees leadership skills in you. That's a great thing and Chester are going to be successful", Wilbur said.

"Our children are doing well too. Wilbur Junior just went away for basic training in the United States Army and our daughter Rene is recently married. She moved to Minnesota with her husband Jeff and she accepted a job offer up there and we're so proud of them", Mary said, glowing.

"You should be", Shelia said.

"Well, it looks like the church service is about to start. I think that we should begin making our way inside", Lucas suggested.

"Yes, we should", Wilbur agreed.

Everyone enters the church and when they walk in, the church choir is singing "Oh Happy Day." The choir and church members are singing and clapping their hands with joy and praise. Lucas and his family join in and start clapping as well, while looking for some vacant seating, with Wilbur Senior and Mary Baxley following them. They see some unclaimed seats in the middle of the church and walk toward them. A short time later, they all sit down next to each other and five minutes later, Pastor Larry Wilkins walks in and makes his way toward a light brown podium. He's carrying his Bible in his left hand and waves to his congregation with his right hand. When Pastor Wilkins reaches his podium, he places his Bible on it and then turns around briefly and faces the choir. Pastor Wilkins claps his hands and then salutes them and then he turns back around and opens his Bible. He thumbs through the pages in search of the book of Isaiah, Chapter forty-one. When he finds it, he patiently waits for the choir to finish singing and then addresses his congregation. Pastor Wilkins motions his arms and up and down and instructs everyone to be seated and they obey him. Two hours later, Pastor Wilkins has the entire congregation in a spiritual frenzy with his fire and brimstone sermon. The choir is singing their hearts out and the music in the background is heartwarming and the musicians are masterfully executing their keys. Pastor Wilkins is communicating how awesome and great God is, he's thanking God for his blessings, and is praying for church members to be blessed. His chocolate bald head is sweating uncontrollably and sweat is running down the sides of his face like Niagara Falls. He takes a handkerchief and uses it in an effort to dry his face, while some members are waving their arms and hands and praising God. Other members are pumping their fists heavenward and yelling, "Thank you Jesus!" or fanning their faces. Still, other congregation members are stomping their feet and jumping up and down, while others are yelling with joy, with tears rolling down their cheeks. The choir is singing at the top of their lungs and the church has an intimate feeling of a waterfall of love, praise, and joy for God. Toward the end of the church service, a collection plate is passed around and members contribute to it. Not long after the collection plate is filled, the church service ends and Pastor Wilkins wishes everyone a blessed day. Some church members rise up and make their way toward the exit while others mull around and catch up on old times. Several people stay and talk with Pastor Wilkins about his sermon and ask him questions. Lucas and the boys start to make their way toward the exit, but Shelia taps Lucas on the shoulder and talks him and the boys into staying. Shelia wants Lucas to talk with Pastor Wilkins and he reluctantly agrees and they walk over to him while Chester and Melvin talk to some girls that they recognize. As they're walking toward him, Lucas and Shelia are holding hands and as they're approaching Pastor Wilkins, a young couple is walking away. When Pastor Wilkins sees Lucas and Shelia, his face breaks out into a pleasant smile and then he speaks.

"Lucas and Shelia, it's great to see y' all. How's the family? How have y' all been?", Pastor Wilkins asked.

"We're fine Pastor Wilkins and what about you and your family?", Shelia asked.

"We've been okay. Lucas, I'm happy that you still remember how to get to our church", Pastor Wilkins joked.

"I know that it has been a while since I've been here", Lucas said, wanting to crawl into a hole.

"Yes, but at least you're here now. No matter what, you can always come back home."

"You still deliver great sermons and they're so powerful and inspirational."

"Thank you Lucas and I'm just trying to do my best to preach the Word of God."

"Pastor Wilkins, how is your wife Michelle? Does she still volunteer to help the homeless at the Center City Rescue Mission?", Shelia asked.

"Yes she does Shelia. Unfortunately, she's not here today because she's feeling under the weather. I think that she might have the flu, but I'm praying that she doesn't."

"We pray that she feels better."

"On my way home, I'm going to stop off at Walgreens and pick her up some Cold and Flu medicine."

"Pastor Wilkins, do you still play a good game of pool?", Lucas asked.

"That's difficult for me to say because I haven't played pool in a while. I've been so busy lately that I haven't had much free time", Pastor Wilkins said.

"I understand where you're coming from."

"I'm glad that y' all showed up and don't be a stranger to the church."

"I won't and I promise that I'll attend church more often", Lucas promised.

"Shelia, I'm going to trust you to make sure that I see Lucas more often", Pastor Wilkins said, joking.

"You can trust me", Shelia said, laughing.

"Great."

"Pastor Wilkins, we're going to leave now and have a blessed rest of the day", Lucas said, shaking his hand.

"Right back at y' all. Buckle up and drive home safely."

"I will and good-bye Pastor Wilkins."

"Good-bye."

Lucas and Shelia walk away and look around for Chester and Melvin and when they see them, they motion for them for to come over. When they're standing next to them, Lucas tells them that they're leaving and the family walks out and heads home.

CHAPTER TWO

Chance Encounter

It's a beautiful, sunny, April afternoon and the temperature is in the fifties. It's the weekend and Lucas and Shelia are quietly watching Living Single on television. During a commercial break, Lucas gets up you and goes to use the bathroom and when he's finished, Shelia also decides to use it. When she comes back, Shelia is obviously irritated. Lucas notices this and asks her what's wrong.

"Lucas, you left up the toilet flap again."

"So what's really bothering you?", Lucas asked.

"You've been doing that a lot lately and I'm sick and tired of it. It only takes a couple of seconds to put the toilet flap down."

"You're serious and I can't believe that you're being this petty. I'm your husband, not your housekeeper."

"Why would you say something like that? I know that you're my husband."

"Are you watching my every move now?"

"Lucas, you're being silly and you've had a piss poor attitude lately and I don't like it", Shelia said, firmly.

"I don't need for you or anyone else to tell me about the condition of my attitude. I'm a man and I don't need you to tell me how I should behave or what to do", Lucas said, defensively.

"What's wrong with you Lucas? I've never questioned your manhood and why would you suggest something like that?"

"Just because you're the breadwinner of our family right now doesn't mean that you can say anything to me. I'm still the man of this house Shelia Lightfoot", Lucas said, pounding a table.

"What? You mean that you're upset that I'm working Lucas? Really? Should I quit and let our bills pile up? What should I do instead Lucas?", Shelia said, placing her hands on her hips, defiantly.

"We still have money in the bank and I'm still receiving Unemployment Insurance. You're not the only one paying bills and you should respect the fact that I'm your husband."

"I'm going to always respect the fact that you're my husband and that's never going to change. You're our sons' father and you're letting your pride get the best of you. If you don't get it under control, it's going to eventually tear our family apart", Shelia said.

"I don't want that", Lucas said, horrified.

"Lucas, you have to stop feeling sorry for yourself. There are people in this world that have a much worse situation than yours. You have a family that loves and supports you and some people don't have that."

"You make some good points."

"We're a team Lucas and just lean on me right now. Swallow your pride and this will turn out okay for us", Shelia assured him.

"I appreciate that Shelia and I apologize for the terrible things that I said. I promise that I'll help out a lot more around the house", Lucas said.

"Thank you Lucas and I appreciate you saying that."

"Shelia, I'm so frustrated and I'm not used to not working. Sometimes, I feel useless, embarrassed, and depressed."

"Just continue your job search and eventually you'll get a job. Don't give up Lucas."

"I won't. I'll wake up early tomorrow morning and surf the Internet for job opportunities like never before", Lucas promised.

"Great! That's the spirit!", Shelia said, excitedly.

They talk for another half an hour and the rest of the day is peaceful. The following morning, Lucas is surfing the Internet and researching various employment websites. He comes across a job opening for a supervisor at the B. Mitchell Candy Company in Butlerville, Illinois on www.illinoisjobs.com that interests him. Lucas studies the qualifications and he believes that his skills and experience would be a good match and sends them his resume. He sees two other companies that interest him and sends them resumes as well and later that day, Lucas updates Shelia on the progress of his job search.

"Shelia, I've seen some good job opportunities and I feel better about my chances of landing a job", Lucas said, gleefully.

"That's wonderful", Shelia said.

"One company really stood out and I applied for their supervisor position."

"What's the name of the company and where is it located?"

"The name of the company is the B. Mitchell Candy Company and they're located in Butlerville."

"That's about half an hour from Center City."

"Yes and they're accepting resumes all week and I already sent mine. The early bird gets the worm, or in my case, the early resume gets the job", Lucas said.

"That's a great line Lucas and I love your positive thinking. I pray that they hire you", Shelia said, hopeful.

"So do I and I'm hoping that they call me sometime next week for an interview."

"That would be nice. I forgot to ask you Lucas, what are the hours of this job?'

"It's a first shift supervisor position and the hours are from eight a.m. until four-thirty p.m. and that would be convenient for our family. We would be working different shifts, but one of us would always be here to keep an eye on the home front."

"You're right."

"There were other companies that I checked out and they looked promising as well", Lucas said.

"Lucas, keep me informed and I'll ask my co-workers and friends about possible job leads", Shelia said.

"Thank you sweet cakes for all your encouragement", Lucas said, planting a kiss on her.

"You're welcome honey", Shelia said, kissing him back.

They spend the rest of the day relaxing and enjoying each other and the boys and the following afternoon, Lucas and Shelia are lying in bed and watching television. Suddenly, the phone rings and Lucas leans toward their nightstand and see that one of his parents is calling. He picks up the phone and answers it.

"Hello", Lucas said.

"Hello Lucas, this is your loving mother. How are you and your family?", Mom said.

"Mom, it's great hearing your voice and your loving son is doing just fine. My family is doing okay and how are you and Dad?"

"Your father and I are doing great."

"I'm happy to hear that."

"Lucas, are you and Shelia busy?", Mom asked.

"No Mom. What's up?", Lucas asked.

"Well, your father and I were talking about getting out of the house. If y' all wasn't busy, we would love to come over."

"We would love to see you and Dad Mom. When did you and Dad want to come through?", Lucas asked.

"What time would be best for you and Shelia?", Mom asked.

"We're just relaxing today Mom, so anytime would be fine."

"What about five o' clock this evening?"

"That's fine and we'll see you and Dad then."

"Okay Lucas and we'll see y' all then. We love y' all and good-bye", Mom said.

"We love y' all too and good-bye", Lucas said.

Later that evening, Aaron and Denise Lightfoot show up and Lucas answers the front door. He hugs his parents and then escorts them inside and Lucas points toward some coat hangers and indicates that they can hang their coats and on them and they thank Lucas. Aaron helps Denise remove her coat and she thanks him and they wink at each other and a short time later, they enter the living room, holding hands and their eyes light up when they see Shelia. All three of them hug and embrace each other and when they're finished, Lucas and Shelia encourage them to sit down on the living room sofa and they both sit down. Moments later, Lucas and Shelia sit down next to each other and everyone is happy and excited to see each other. Shelia has brewed a cup of coffee and asks them if they would like a cup.

"That's so nice of you Shelia and yes I would love a cup", Denise said.

"Me too Shelia and thank you", Aaron said.

"Y' all are welcome and it's pretty cold outside. Do y' all want your coffee black or with some creamer?', Shelia asked.

"I'll take two spoons of sugar and one spoonful of creamer."

"And I just want my coffee black."

"Okay, I'll be right back", Shelia said.

"Thanks again Shelia."

"No problem."

Five minutes later, Shelia comes back into the living room and hands them their coffee and they graciously accept it. They both take a couple of sips and then place their cups on the living room table. A short time later, Aaron asks where Chester and Melvin are.

"They're in their room and let me call them out here. Chester! Melvin! Your grandparents are here!" Lucas said.

"Maybe they're busy", Denise reasoned.

"They're not too busy to see their grandparents. Boys come on out here!"

Chester and Melvin come out of their rooms and they break out into loving smiles as they approach their grandparents. They embrace and hug each other tightly and Denise kisses them on their foreheads. Moments later, they stare at Chester and Melvin with pride and joy and then Denise shakes her head and then speaks to the boys.

"I can't believe how you boys have grown and it seems like yesterday that you were babies", Denise said, glowing.

"The years go by so fast and they'll be young adults before we know it", Aaron said.

"Yes, but there not quite there yet", Lucas said, jokingly.

"Lucas, they're both taller than you and I'm a little surprised."

"You just had to bring that up didn't you Dad? And why are you surprised?"

"Calm down Lucas. You know that we don't have many tall family members", Aaron said.

"You're right."

"Chester definitely has the height and he's put it to great use on the basketball court", Shelia said.

"Chester, your grandpa was a starting point guard in high school", Lucas said.

"Really?"

"Yes and I was a decent player."

"Coach Jenkins believes that I have the talent to earn a college basketball scholarship. He played at his alma mater, Chicago State University and he's good friends with their head coach. Bradley University and the University of Northern Iowa have also shown interest in me."

"Keep on working hard Chester and good things will happen for you."

"I'm the captain of my debate team and Coach Hamilton thinks that we have a chance to win the conference championship this year", Melvin said, proudly.

"You're the captain? That's impressive and we're proud of you", Denise said.

"Thank you."

"You've always been a Brainiac and that's why I gave you the nickname, "professor"", Aaron said.

"I hope that you never stop calling me that because I always get a kick out of it", Melvin said.

"You never have to worry about that Melvin", Aaron said.

"Chester and Melvin, I can imagine that both of you are popular with the girls. Do y' all have girlfriends?" Aaron asked.

"Well, I'm seeing this girl named Melanie and we've been seeing each other for a while now", Chester said, blushing.

"I've never seen a young black man's face turn so red"; Denise joked.

Everyone busts out laughing and when they finally calm down, Aaron looks in Melvin's direction and speaks to him.

"How about you Melvin? Do you have a girlfriend?"

"Yes Grandpa and her name is Cindy."

"None of us should be surprised that the girls like our sons because they're handsome just like they're father", Lucas said, smiling and puffing out his chest.

"I think that I might have had something to do with that", Shelia said, winking at Lucas and folding her arms.

"I didn't forget about you Shelia", Lucas said, smiling.

"And their grandparents have something to do with that too", Denise said.

"Chester and Melvin are outstanding young men and we're so proud of them", Aaron said.

They talk for another fifteen minutes and then Aaron pulls Lucas to the side and encourages him to come to the Liquor Store with him. Lucas accepts his invitation and before they leave, Lucas and Aaron ask everyone if they want anything back. Denise indicates that she doesn't need anything and Chester and Melvin don't want anything. Shelia asks them to bring her back some two for a dollar Cheeto Cheese Puffs, her favorite candy bar, a Snickers, and a can of Sprite. Lucas tells her that they will and Shelia tells Lucas to wait while she goes and gets the money. Lucas waves her off and lets her know that he'll pay for her items and Shelia thanks him. Minutes later, they pull up in front of Carl's Liquor Store and they both get out and walk in. They scan the various beers that are available and Aaron asks Lucas what beer that he wants. Lucas tells him that he has a tasty craving for Miller Genuine Draft and Aaron picks up a four-pack of the beer. They walk to the counter and he pulls out a twenty-dollar bill out of his right pants pocket. He hands the bill over to the cashier and then the cashier gives him his change. A short time later, Lucas orders Shelia's items and purchases himself a box of Salem Slim Lights Cigarettes. As Lucas is reaching into his pocket to pull out his money, his father tells him to keep his money because he's going to pay for everything. Lucas is pleasantly surprised and thanks him and moments later, they walk out and when they arrive back at Lucas' house, Aaron turns the car off. He tells Lucas that he wants to have a conversation with him.

"Sure Dad. What do you want to talk about?", Lucas asked.

"Lucas, I know how you're feeling and going through with your employment situation", Aaron said.

"You've been talking to Shelia, haven't you?"

"Yes, and she's been concerned about you. But even if I had not talked to her, I would've known what you've been feeling Lucas. I've been through tough times too and my life has not always been peaches and cream."

"Dad, you're so right and this situation is messing with my manhood. I'm supposed to be the breadwinner of my family and sometimes, I feel so damn helpless!", Lucas said.

"Lucas, I know that not working is frustrating for you", Aaron said.

"It sure is!"

"You shouldn't feel less than a man Lucas because this situation isn't your fault. In Shelia, you have a damn good wife and she's going to help you have the strength to get through this. She has always been in your corner and will continue to be."

"She has been great to me and Shelia has been a wonderful mother to Chester and Melvin."

"Don't give up Lucas and pray and be patient. Things will turn around for you and I have a strong feeling that you'll be employed again soon", Aaron said, patting him on the shoulder.

"Okay. Dad, I feel so much better after this conversation that we've had. You really lifted my spirits and life looks better to me and thank you", Lucas said.

"You're welcome Lucas and don't hesitate to call us if you and your family need anything."

"I will."

"Good. Lucas, did you want to split this beer? We can both have two beers a piece."

"I would love to go in half and half with my father."

"Same here son. I think that we should go in the house now before everyone begins to worry about us", Aaron suggested.

"I agree", Lucas said, nodding his head.

They get out of the car and go into the house and everyone continues talking for another half an hour. Then Aaron announces that they're leaving and Lucas and Shelia say that they enjoyed their company. They indicate to Lucas and Shelia that they enjoyed their company as well and then head home. The rest of the day is uneventful and a week later, Lucas and Shelia are huddled together on the living room sofa and they're watching Maury. When Maury goes off, Shelia turns toward Lucas and tells him that she has a surprise for him.

"You do? What is it?", Lucas asked.

"It wouldn't be a surprise if I told you", Shelia said.

"Good point", Lucas said, smacking a hand against his forehead.

"Just hold on a minute and I'll show you. I'll be right back", Shelia said.

"Okay."

Shelia gets up off the sofa and goes into their bedroom and closes the door behind her. She opens their closet door and bends over and moves around some bags and old clothes and finally sees what she's searching for. Shelia takes out a Weber Original Kettle Charcoal Grill and walks back into the living room and Lucas cannot believe his eyes. Moments later, Shelia gives him the grill box and he reads the features of the grill and then Lucas places the box on the floor and hugs and kisses Shelia. Lucas tells Shelia how much he appreciates her gift and Shelia tells Lucas that she loves him. Moments later, Lucas speaks.

"Shelia, this gift was the last thing that I expected and it has made my day", Lucas said.

"Lucas, I know that things have been difficult for you and I wanted to lift your spirits. And I know how much you love to grill and that other grill has seen its best days", Shelia said.

"This makes me feel so much better. It's almost as if you read my mind because I was thinking about buying another one."

"Nothing lasts forever and our grill needed to be upgraded."

"You definitely know me."

"We make a great team."

"We sure do and I love this grill because it comes with a one-touch cleaning system. Cleaning up after grilling can be a pain in the butt and this will make that easier for me. I love it", Lucas said.

"I'm happy that you love it Lucas", Shelia said.

"And I won't have to worry as much about the temperature of the grill. The dampers will allow me to concentrate more on grilling."

"I already know that you're going to do more grilling this summer."

"You better believe it!"

"I noticed those features too and I was impressed, so I bought it", Shelia said.

"I can't wait until the summer so that I can grill some great foods. Maybe we can have a cookout this summer with our family, friends, and neighbors."

"That would be nice Lucas and it has been a while since we've had one."

"It has been about two or three years."

"That long? We're overdue."

"I agree."

Nothing special happens for the rest of the day. Three days later, on a Wednesday afternoon, Lucas is home watching The Steve Harvey Show in their living room. Suddenly, the phone rings and he rise up from the sofa and leans and walks over to the phone and picks it up. Lucas recognizes the number as B. Mitchell and answers it.

"Hello."

"Hello, may I speak with Lucas Lightfoot?"

"Speaking."

"Mr. Lightfoot, my name is Tommy Madison and I'm the Plant Manager at B. Mitchell. We received your resume and would love for you to come in for an interview. Are you interested?", Tommy asked.

"Thank you for calling and I'm definitely interested", Lucas said.

"Are you available to come in for an interview tomorrow afternoon?"

"Yes I can."

"Can you come in at one o' clock?"

"I sure can."

"Good. Lucas, when you arrive here, park in the visitors section of our company parking lot. And when you walk into the front entrance, tell our receptionist Judy Thompson that you're here for your job interview. And make sure that you sign our visitors sheet", Tommy warned.

"Okay", Lucas said.

"Do you have any questions Lucas?", Tommy asked.

"No and I'll see you then", Lucas said.

"Okay, I'll see you tomorrow and good-bye."

"Good-bye."

Lucas hangs up with a huge smile on his face and he can't wait to tell Shelia the good news. He resumes watching The Steve Harvey Show and the rest of the day is standard procedure. Later that night, Lucas greets Shelia warmly as she walks in from her work day.

"I'm happy that you're home Shelia and how was your day?", Lucas asked.

"It was a rough day. We had some new workers on the assembly line and they slowed production and we had to stop the line quite a few times. And on top of that, my supervisor got on my last nerves", Shelia said, letting out a long sigh.

"Well, forget about this day Shelia, it's over. I'm pretty sure that tomorrow will be much better", Lucas said.

"I hope so."

"I cooked and fixed you a plate of food and it's in the refrigerator covered with aluminum foil. It's sitting on top and next to the milk.

I fixed chicken, macaroni and cheese and some string beans. And there's a twelve-pack of your favorite soda, Pepsi in there too."

"That's so thoughtful of you Lucas and I appreciate it. I'm starved."

"I know how it feels when you come home from a hard day of work. And the boys loved the food and I wish that you could've seen the looks on their faces."

"Well Lucas, you're a pretty good cook."

"Thank you Shelia."

"You're welcome."

"I have some great news Shelia."

"What is it Lucas?"

"B. Mitchell called me today and they want me to come in for an interview tomorrow afternoon!", Lucas said, excitedly.

"That's great news and I'm so happy for you! I've been praying for you and I knew that things would start looking up for you!", Shelia said, thrilled.

"I just hope that I give a good interview and I'm nervous about that."

"Don't worry about that Lucas because you're going to ace the interview."

"I hope so", Lucas said, crossing his fingers.

"You will", Shelia said, confidently.

"I'm going to wear a suit and tie tomorrow and make sure that I'm smelling good."

"When they see you looking and smelling good, they might hire you on the spot", Shelia teased.

"It would be nice if it was that easy", Lucas said, smiling.

"You have to think positive."

"Good point."

"Lucas, I'm going to eat your great food and then freshen up before joining you in the bedroom", Shelia said.

"Looking forward to it", Lucas said.

They exchange kisses and go their separate ways. After Shelia finishes eating and freshening up, she joins Lucas and he's lying comfortably in their bed watching Dish Nation on television. He smiles when he sees Shelia and she returns the smile and after changing into her pajamas, she climbs into bed. They watch television for an hour before they both decide that it's time to go to sleep. But before they do, Shelia suggests that they pray and Lucas agrees. They climb out of bed and walk toward the front edge of it and they hold hands and kneel down on their knees. They close their eyes tightly and Shelia leads them in prayer and she prays that God will protect their family and bless them with good health and prosperity. And she prays that Lucas will be blessed to give a successful job interview. When she's finished, they both say, "Amen" and they open their eyes and lift each other up and climb back into bed. A short time later, they both fall asleep and the next day, Lucas has just exited the highway on his way to B. Mitchell. He makes a right turn and begins driving on Robert E. Lee Boulevard, which is the main street of Butlerville. When he's almost at B. Mitchell, his car stops at a red light and Lucas studies his surroundings. He looks toward his passengers' side and sees a Confederate Flag and it shocks him. Lucas tries to calm his nerves and remind himself that he is well schooled in self-defense. His father and grandfather served honorably in the United States Army and faced racism that he could only imagine. He remembered the horrible stories that they shared with him about the brutal violence and humiliation that blacks experienced. They taught Lucas how to box and took him to the shooting range as a young man and he became pretty accurate. If any racist people tried to harm him or his family, they were going to pay a painful price. If necessary, he could legally pump some bullets into their asses because he has a legal Conceal and Carry Permit. He tells himself that he's just as much an American as them and he is not going to let anyone scare or intimidate him. Lucas is jarred out of his reflective thoughts when he hears someone honking their horn behind him and he sees that the stoplight has turned green. Lucas proceeds driving again and several minutes later, Lucas pulls into the B. Mitchell visitors parking lot. A short time later, he enters the building and Lucas walks toward the receptionists' desk and Judy Thompson is behind it and he tells her that he's there for his interview. Judy tells Lucas to sign the visitor's sheet, which he does, and then Judy encourages him to have a seat in the visitor's lobby while she contacts Tommy. Lucas sits down on a sofa and to occupy his time, he picks up a copy of Forbes Magazine from a small table and begins reading. Five minutes later, a bald, middle-aged white man comes out and he has blue eyes and a neatly trimmed mustache. He has big ears and a huge nose, a large forehead, and he has a slim build and looks as if he could've run track in his youth. Judy informs him that Lucas is waiting for him and Tommy thanks her and then approaches Lucas. When he's near Lucas, he looks up from his magazine and Tommy greets him and Lucas puts down the magazine. He rises up from the sofa and they exchange firm handshakes and then Tommy instructs Lucas to follow him into his office. When they're inside, he encourages Lucas to sit down in a chair in front of his desk. Lucas occupies the chair while Tommy walks around to the back of his desk and sits down. Moments later, Tommy begins the interview.

"Lucas, I want you to tell me about yourself", Tommy said.

"Well, I graduated from Center City High School and I love playing pool and bowling. I'm also a huge Chicago Bears fan and my all-time favorite player is Mike Singletary", Lucas said.

"Pool is a great game and I love playing it."

"Yes it is and I enjoy it too."

"What are your greatest strengths and weaknesses?"

"My greatest strengths are my leadership skills and ability to motivate employees. My biggest weaknesses is that I demand excellence and sometimes I overdo it and rub employees the wrong way. Sometimes, I can be a little insensitive."

"Why should our company hire you?"

"You should hire me because I'm an experienced supervisor that has shown that I can help a company make money. I was named the Supervisor of the Year more than once at Martha's and I have proven that I'm loyal, dependable, and reliable."

"What are your salary expectations?", Tommy asked.

"Well, when I researched the position, I noticed that it paid fourteen to sixteen dollars an hour, depending on someone's experience", Lucas said.

"That's right."

"My salary expectation is sixteen dollars an hour."

"Okay. What is your proudest achievement?"

"Being named the Supervisor of the Year and my attendance record."

"That's quite an accomplishment. Lucas, our interview is pretty much over and do you have any questions?", Tommy asked.

"Yes I do. Can you tell me when I might be notified of my interview status?", Lucas asked.

"Probably within the next couple of weeks. Anything else?"

"Not that I can think of."

"Well Lucas, have a great rest of the day", Tommy said, rising up from his chair.

"Thank you and you do the same", Lucas said, as they shake hands. He exits Tommy's office as he calls in another job applicant and Lucas leaves and heads toward his car. When he's inside, he buckles his seat belt and Lucas hears his stomach growling. He decides to stop off at the Mc Donald's that he drove past on his way to his interview. He starts up his car and begins driving and a short time later, he pulls into the Mc Donald's parking lot. Lucas considers ordering his food through the Drive Thru, but has a change of heart and decides to order and eat inside. When he walks inside, an uneasy, unwelcome feeling comes over him. He scans the restaurant in various directions and notices that he's the only black person in there. The customers are white and some of them eyeball Lucas suspiciously and Lucas can sense the resentment that his presence has created, but he ignores it. He walks up to the counter and orders a number one Big Mac Meal. After receiving his tray of food, Lucas walks over to a counter and lays down his tray grabs some napkins, ketchup packets, and a straw for his Coca-Cola. He places the items on his tray and cautiously picks it up and walks slowly toward a table. When he arrives at the table, Lucas places the tray on it and sits down and prays before he begins eating. When he's finished, he begins eating his meal while enjoying the scenery outside. Five minutes later, a short, middle-aged white woman suddenly screams frantically and everyone looks around to see what's happening. A tall, middle-aged white man is holding his throat with both hands and his face is turning red. The woman yells out for help.

"I think that my husband is choking! I think that my husband is choking! Somebody please help us!"

Lucas sprints up from his seat and rushes over to them and begins performing the Heinrich Maneuver on the man. Lucas stands behind him and places a leg in between his and then wraps his arms around him, just above the stomach. He makes a fist with his right hand and grabs on to it with his left hand and Lucas thrusts inward and outward. Moments later, some food comes out and minutes later, the man is standing upright and he concentrates on regaining his normal breathing pattern. When he does, the man and woman thank Lucas for saving his life. Lucas assures them that it was no problem and suggests to the man that he get checked out and by a doctor. He declines, but the man picks up a cup of Sprite from his tray and takes a couple of big sips. He then places it back on the tray and the woman hugs the man and kisses him for what seems like forever. Everyone in the restaurant stands up and gives Lucas a standing ovation and they clap their hands and cheer. When the cheering stops, everyone sits down and resumes eating their food. A short time later, the man strikes up a conversation with Lucas.

"Sir, I owe you a debt of gratitude and I'll never forget you", he said, shaking Lucas' hand.

"Neither will I because you saved my husband's life", she said, gratefully.

"Well, if I was in that situation, I would hope that someone would help me", Lucas said.

"You're being too modest and you're a hero. I'm sorry sir, we forgot to introduce ourselves and I'm Mayor Dugan Lane of Butlerville and this is my wife, Karen. It's nice to meet you."

"And my name is Lucas Lightfoot and I'm from Center City. It's nice to meet both of you."

"We've never seen you in our town before. May I ask what brings you here?"

"Well, I just finished interviewing for a supervisor position at B. Mitchell."

"Really? I know some people that work there and good luck to you", Mayor Lane said.

"Thank you. It's a small world", Lucas said.

"What are you eating?"

"A number one Big Mac Meal."

"Well, you're going to have another one on me."

"Thank you and that's so generous of you."

"It's the least that I can do after what you did for me. I want to give you my business card and call me anytime. If I can be of assistance, let me know", Mayor Lane said.

"Thank you Mayor Lane and I appreciate this", Lucas said, putting his card into his pocket.

"If I'm unavailable, leave a message with my secretary Maria Stanford and she'll relay it to me."

"Okay, let me give you my phone number Mayor Lane. Do you have a pen and paper on you?", Lucas asked.

"I have a pen and I can write your name and phone number on this napkin. What is it?", Mayor Lane said, removing a pen from his shirt pocket.

"It's area code two one seven, five six two, thirty-seven fifty-five."

"Say that one more time Lucas", Mayor Lane said, leaning over on the table and writing it on the napkin.

"Area code two one seven, five six two, thirty-seven fifty-five", Lucas said.

"I got it."

The mayor puts Lucas' number into his shirt pocket along with his pen. Lucas puts the mayor's business card into his pants pocket. Lucas continues talking to Mayor Lane and his wife Karen for several more minutes before Lucas excuses himself to finish his meal. He's almost finished his meal when Mayor Lane and Karen approach his table and he places the Big Mac Meal next to Lucas' tray and he thanks him. The Mayor and Karen smile at him and then they walk out. Five minutes later, Lucas finishes his meal and heads home and two weeks later, Lucas and Shelia are home. They're listening to various musical artists on the radio. They're snapping their fingers and dancing and grooving to the music when suddenly, the phone rings. Lucas goes to see whom it is and the B. Mitchell phone number is showing up. He asks Shelia to turn down the radio and she complies and Lucas answers it.

"Hello", Lucas said.

"This is Tommy Madison and I'm the Plant Manager at the B. Mitchell Candy Company. May I speak with Lucas Lightfoot?", Tommy asked.

"This is him Tommy."

"Good afternoon Lucas and how are you?"

"I'm fine and you?"

"I'm good. Lucas, I'm calling to congratulate you on being hired for our Supervisor Position. Welcome aboard to our company and we look forward to working with you", Tommy said.

"I received the job? Thank you and I look forward to working with B. Mitchell", Lucas said, barely able to contain his excitement.

"Lucas, I was blown away by your resume and job interview. You have one of the best resumes that I've ever seen!"

"Thank you."

"Mayor Dugan Lane told me great things about you."

"What? You know Mayor Lane?", Lucas asked, shocked.

"I sure do. We've been good friends since high school and he's a good man", Tommy said.

"What a coincidence."

"Lucas, you indicated to me wanted to work first shift. Can you come in Monday morning for orientation?"

"Yes I can."

"Great. And by the way Lucas, we're going to pay you the maximum salary of sixteen dollars an hour."

"Thank you."

"And Lucas, I know that your work hours are from eight o' clock a.m. until four-thirty p.m., but I want you to be here at seven a.m. Monday. I'll guide you through a tour of the plant and you'll have to fill out some paperwork."

"I'll be there", Lucas said.

"And of course, you know that working every other weekend is mandatory", Tommy reminded him.

"Yes I know."

"When you show up, tell Judy that you're there for orientation and she'll notify me."

"Alright."

"Well, Lucas, congratulations again, and I'll see you Monday morning. Good-bye."

"See you then Tommy. Good-bye."

Lucas hangs up and his face breaks out into a Kool-Aid smile as does Shelia and she congratulates him. They embrace and hug each other tightly and then kiss each other on numerous parts of their faces. Moments later, Shelia begins talking to him.

"Lucas, I told you things were going to look up for you! I had a strong feeling that you were going to get that job!", Shelia said.

"I'm so happy that you were right!", Lucas said.

"We never lost faith and God pulled us through."

"He sure did."

"When do you start Lucas?"

"They want me to come in Monday morning for orientation, but I don't when I will officially start."

"Great for you."

"I'm happy that it's a first shift position and I'll be a supervisor again! You were right Shelia about being let go at Martha's could be a blessing in disguise. They're going to pay me sixteen dollars an hour!"

"I'm just so happy for you right now Lucas", Shelia said.

"I'm happy for our family and now things can go back to normal. I hated being unemployed so much", Lucas said.

"It's been a great day."

Later that evening, Chester and Melvin are visiting friends and Lucas and Shelia are at home. They're huddled together in their bedroom and watching one of their favorite television show, Black Lightning. When it goes off, Shelia is in a horny mood and she reaches out her right hand and begins massaging Lucas' crotch. He's slightly startled and when he recovers from the shock, he looks into her seductive eyes. and begins enjoying the massage and his face breaks out into a huge smile. Then Shelia unbuttons Lucas' pants and then cautiously unzips them and pulls his drawers toward her and pulls out his rock-hard penis. Shelia massages it up and down and sideways and then spits on it a couple of times and then resumes massaging his steel pole. A short time later, Shelia gets on her knees and begins sucking Lucas' dick and he closes his eyes and moans with delight and savors every suck. While Shelia's head is bobbing up and down, Lucas places his right hand on Shelia's donkey booty and rubs it in a circular motion. Shelia sucks his hot dog for several minutes and then Lucas suggests that they get naked and Shelia readily agrees. After they've removed their clothes, they both climb back into the bed. Lucas indicates to Shelia that he wants her to get into the doggy style position and she does so. He carefully inserts his hot dog into her flaming hot pussy and moments later, Lucas begins working his dick like a well-oiled machine. He occasionally spanks her ass and this turns her on even more and Shelia encourages Lucas to pump her even harder and he complies. Fifteen minutes later, Lucas tells Shelia that he wants his pole sucked some more and he lays on his back with a pillow under his head and neck. Shelia resumes sucking Lucas' dick and then she lifts up his brick hard dick and occasionally goes down on his balls and Lucas moans with joy. Minutes later, she works her way back to sucking his dick and after a while, they switch into the missionary position. Lucas works his tongue like a surgeon on her clit and Shelia's body begins to quiver uncontrollably. He then gently inserts his middle finger into her warm pussy and sweet waterfall juices begin to overflow his finger. Moments later, Lucas tells Shelia to raise her legs up and then he inserts his hot dog into her wanting pussy and he smoothly works his hips back and forth.

Occasionally, she crosses her legs and ankles, while holding her legs with both hands. Lucas has his hands balled up in fists flat on the bed on the outside of her legs in an effort to create more dick leverage. He pumps his pipe in and out of Shelia's pussy for another half an hour and then he feels himself getting ready to release his white, creamy load. He tells Shelia that he's about to cum and pulls out his dick and creams all over her stomach and moans while jerking his dick. When Lucas is finished, he lets out a sigh of joyous relief and a smile comes across his face as well as Shelia's. They lay in the bed for some time and relax and catch their breaths. When Lucas and Shelia compose themselves and gather their thoughts, they exchange passionate kisses and hugs. Then they both get up and walk toward the shower holding hands and enter and clean each other up. When they're finished, they put on their pajamas and they get in their bed and resume watching television. They conversate with each other until they both fall asleep.

Chapter Three

No Fear

It's Monday morning and Lucas has arrived at B. Mitchell. He is entering the front entrance and he walks up to the receptionist Judy and tells her that he's there for his orientation. She says good morning and greets him with a warm smile and congratulates him on receiving the supervisor's position.

"Thank you Judy and I didn't think that you would remember me", Lucas said, surprised.

"You're welcome and I remember how nice you were", Judy said.

"I know that I have to sign the visitor's sheet, so I'll do that right now", Lucas said, picking up an ink pen.

"Tommy is on the plant floor right now and let me try and get in touch with him. In the meantime, Lucas, you can have a seat."

"Alright."

After signing the sheet, Lucas walks over to a sofa and sits down and patiently waits for Tommy to come out. Ten minutes later, Tommy comes out to Lucas and greets him with a smile and they exchange handshakes. Tommy apologizes to Lucas for taking so long and Lucas waves him off and accepts his apology and then Tommy proceeds to escort Lucas on a company tour. Before they reach the plant floor, Tommy shows Lucas where the bathrooms and the employee break rooms are. Then they walk into the employees' locker room and Tommy explains to Lucas some things that he needs to know.

"Lucas, when you come in every morning, pick one of these blue aprons to put on. They indicate that you're a supervisor and the red aprons are for our regular employees. The lockers in that corner are designated for supervisors", Tommy said, pointing toward them.

"That's simple enough, Lucas said.

"And before you go out to the plant floor, make sure that your employees have on hair and beard nets. Also make sure that they're wearing plastic gloves."

"Where are those?"

"Follow me and I'll show you", Tommy said, motioning an arm forward.

"Alright", Lucas said.

They leave the locker room and walk a short distance. They see a small cabinet and Tommy opens it and it contains all the necessary employee equipment. Tommy and Lucas put on their hair and beard nets and plastic gloves and then Tommy escorts Lucas to the plant floor. As they're walking, Tommy explains to Lucas how various machines work and their specific functions. Tommy also explains company procedures and introduces him to other supervisors and some employees as they make their way through various departments. As they're walking through the plant, Lucas gradually has an uneasy, uncomfortable feeling that comes over him. He begins to seriously scan the employees and some of them eyeball him suspiciously. Some of them are rolling their eyes and placing their hands on their hips while others whisper to each other and frown at Lucas. Eventually, Lucas shakes off these negative feelings and when the company tour is over, Tommy instructs Lucas to follow him back into his office. When they arrive there, Tommy tells Lucas that he has to fill out some paperwork. When Lucas finishes the paperwork, Tommy asks Lucas if he's ready to begin his first day of work the following day.

"I'm ready and I'm looking forward to it", Lucas said, enthusiastically.

"I'm happy to hear that and I'm looking forward to working with you. I have a good feeling that we're going to get along just fine", Tommy said.

"Me too."

"Lucas, do you have any questions before you leave?"

"Not that I can think of Tommy."

"Well then, Lucas, I'll see you tomorrow. Remember to show up at eight a.m. instead of seven a.m. and don't forget to punch in with your time card."

"Thank you for reminding me Tommy."

"Next week, we'll give you a company card and then you can swipe in when you arrive and leave."

"I'll see you tomorrow Tommy."

"Good-bye Lucas."

"Good-bye Tommy."

They both rise up out of their chairs and firmly shake hands and then Lucas walks out. He says good-bye to Judy on his way home and nothing special happens the rest of the day. A week later, Lucas and his family are eating at Applebee's and they're celebrating Chester signing his National Letter of Intent to attend Bradley University on a college basketball scholarship.

"Chester, we're all so proud of you and congratulations on earning a college basketball scholarship!" Lucas said, excitedly.

"Son, I've been bragging to all our relatives and friends about you!", Shelia said, with her eyes gleaming with pride.

"Well Mom and Dad, I couldn't have done it without your love, support, and encouragement. I'm also thankful to Coach Jenkins for pushing me the way that he did. I didn't always like his methods, but now I realize that he had my best interest at heart", Chester said.

"You've worked hard on and off the court and you deserve every bit of your success."

"I'm proud of you too big brother", Melvin said.

"Thank you Melvin and I'm proud of you too", Chester said.

"These boneless wings are really good, especially with this spinach."

"I love this chicken quesadilla and it's one of my favorite foods."

"Chester, I'm just curious; why did you choose Bradley University?", Lucas asked.

"Well Dad, when I visited their campus, it was beautiful and the people were so friendly. I fell in love with it at first sight."

"You felt welcome there."

"Exactly and I believe that I will receive a great education there. Did y' all know that Bradley University is the only University in the United States that has a school of sports communications?"

"Really? I didn't know that."

"Yes, they do. I've told you and Mom that I would like to pursue a career as a sports broadcaster. This feels like such a perfect fit."

"Chester, you know that your father and I have pushed you and Melvin to get a good education. We're so proud", Shelia said.

"Thank you Mom. Maybe I could become the next Bryant Gumbel or James Brown", Chester said.

"What's wrong with becoming the next Chester Lightfoot?", Lucas asked.

"You make a good point Dad."

"Your father is right. We always want you and Melvin to be yourselves and not like anyone else", Shelia said.

"Mom and Dad, another reason I chose Bradley is because I'll be still in Ilinois. Peoria is only thirty minutes away and it will be much easier for y' all to come watch me play."

"And we're going to definitely watch you play as often as possible."

"I would love that."

"I love this triple chocolate meltdown because I get both cake and ice cream. It's so tasty!", Lucas said.

"I love it too and the shrimp salad because it's so good and healthy!", Shelia said.

"Melvin, you've been too quiet. Are you okay?", Lucas asked.

"I'm alright", Melvin said.

"Your junior year is coming up. Have you started thinking about what career that you might want to pursue?"

"Well, I've seriously thought about becoming a school teacher."

"Really?"

"Dad, why do you sound so surprised?", Melvin asked.

"I didn't mean to offend you Melvin and that's a very admirable profession. I guess that I always viewed you as a Lawyer or Politician", Lucas said.

"I think that I would enjoy being a school teacher more. I love learning and it makes me feel good when I can teach someone how to do something", Melvin said.

"Sounds like a future school teacher to me", Lucas said, smiling.

"This has been a great day for our family", Shelia said.

They continue talking for another forty-five minutes and then decide to leave. Lucas and Sheila leave the waitress a generous tip and she thanks them and the family walks out and heads home. Two weeks later, Lucas is at work and he's walking through the plant and observes his employees. He notices that a couple of them are talking too much and boxes of chocolate are falling off the assembly line. Lucas can see that some of their co-workers are annoyed and he decides to walk over to line seven. Lucas tells the two white men to pay more attention and not to talk so much. They resentfully listen to Lucas and then he walks away and scans other parts of the plant. Twenty minutes later, Lucas walks back to line seven and once again, boxes of chocolate are falling to the ground and Lucas walks over to line seven again. He gives the men a stern lecture about teamwork and they look at Lucas with an irritated look. When Lucas walks away, one of the men rolls his eyes at Lucas, while the other one gives him the finger. Three hours later, during the employees' lunch break, Lucas leaves his office holding his stomach and he can hear it growling. He walks briskly toward the bathroom, almost running, and when he's in there, Lucas closes stall door behind him and locks it. He hurriedly pulls down his pants and sits on the stool and his let out a sigh of relief. Lucas is in there for several minutes when he hears someone coming into the bathroom. He then hears two employees speaking and he recognizes the voices as Charlie Buford and Homer Radcliff.

"Homer, we've got to get rid of that n----- supervisor. I've never taken orders from a chocolate man and this is going to stop", Charlie said, hatefully.

"I agree with you Charlie and we need to get rid of black monkey Lightfoot", Homer said.

In between bowel movements, Lucas leans his body toward the direction of their voices in an effort to listen more clearly to what they're saying.

"We can work together and get rid of chocolate man", Charlie said.

"How? What do you have in mind?", Homer asked, intrigued.

"He's the supervisor, so he's responsible for our level of production, right?"

"Yes, but what are you getting at?"

"We can create some unexpected accidents. We could purposely put the wrong ingredients in the chocolate mixer. Or maybe jam up some of the machines and drastically slow production."

"I love the way that you're thinking Charlie! I also think that we could lie on our daily production sheets that we turn in every day. We could overexaggerate how much product that we've produced."

"And eventually, the higher-ups will look at the company's financial books. They're going to be pointing fingers at him and eventually his ass will be out!"

"We could get other employees to work with us to get monkey Lightfoot out. I love it!"

"Me too. When should we start doing this?", Charlie asked.

"I think that we should start tomorrow. But, today, we can recruit other employees to join our plan", Homer said.

"Sounds like a great plan! Let's do it!"

"Okay!"

Ten minutes after Charlie and Homer leave the bathroom, Lucas comes out of his stall and his face is loaded with anger. He feels his blood boiling throughout his body and a part of him wishes that he could beat up Charlie and Homer. He briefly paces back and forth to let off some steam while trying to figure out what to do about Charlie and Homer. When Lucas has calmed himself down, he lets out a long sigh and then washes his hands and dries them off with paper towels. A short time later, Lucas leaves the bathroom and walks back into his office and reflects on their conversations and what disciplinary action that he should take. Fifteen minutes later, the employee lunch break is over and everyone is gradually making their way back to the plant floor. Lucas is standing next to the plant entrance door waiting for Charlie and Homer to appear. When Lucas sees them, he blocks their path and notifies them that he wants to talk to them in his office. They follow him and when Charlie and Homer enter Lucas' office, he sits down behind his desk and tells them to sit down, which they do. After they're seated, Charlie asks Lucas what's going on.

"Is there something wrong boss? Why are we here?", Charlie asked.

"I've heard both of you making troubling comments", Lucas said, firmly.

"Like what? What are you talking about?"

"I'll get straight to the point gentlemen; I was in the bathroom when y' all made those racist comments about me."

"You must have us mistaken with some other workers", Homer said, defensively.

"I heard the conspiracy plot that both of you were planning against me", Lucas said, looking at them with a cold stare.

"You're wrong and it couldn't have been us."

"Both of my ears work great and I know what I heard."

"I can't believe that you're accusing us of something like that! You're so wrong!", Charlie said, indignant.

"Charlie, don't raise your voice in my office. I'm the man in charge and neither one of you has to concern yourselves with working here anymore. Both of you are fired and I want both of you to clean out your lockers immediately. I'll have security escort y' all from the premises", Lucas said.

"This is absurd!"

"Both of you get out of my office right now!"

Charlie and Homer storm out of Lucas' office and Charlie slams the door behind them. Lucas picks up his phone and calls security and instructs them to escort them off the company grounds. Later that day, during the employees' last lunch break of the day, Lucas addresses his employees about the absence of Charlie and Homer. He also explains his expectations of them.

"I know that everyone is wondering where Charlie and Homer are. They didn't want to cooperate and didn't have the company's best interest at heart, so I fired them. We're all adults and I expect everyone to do their jobs and I expect your best efforts daily. I don't expect everyone to be perfect workers and I realize that you're going to mistakes because we're all human. If you refuse to give your best effort and take pride in your work, then there's the door", Lucas said, pointing toward the exit door.

Lucas clears his throat and looks around the room and then continues speaking.

"Does anyone have any questions or concerns?", Lucas asked, scanning the room.

He notices that Ken Bankart is raising his hand and Lucas acknowledges him and he asks his question.

"Lucas, can we get line number eight fixed? There's too much product spilling on the floor and it's a pain in the butt to clean it up. And the company is losing a lot of money because of this", Ken said.

Lucas smiles approvingly and then answers Ken's question.

"I appreciate you Ken and you're a good company man. Your loyalty and dedication is what B. Mitchell should be about and I'll have a maintenance worker check out your machines after the break. If you're still having problems, I want you to tell me."

"Thank you Lucas and I appreciate that", Ken said.

"You're welcome. Does anyone else have a question?", Lucas asked.

He sees Joyce Haynes raising her hand and Lucas points toward her and nods his head and she asks her question.

"Can we get a television in the break room? It would be nice to be able to watch our favorite television shows while we're eating", Joyce said.

"Joyce, I'm pretty sure that I can arrange that, but let me talk to Tommy. If he approves it, then there will be a television in here", Lucas promised.

"That would be nice."

"Any other questions?", Lucas asked, scanning the room.

Lucas doesn't see anyone raising their hand and he resumes speaking.

"Like I said earlier, I expect everyone to do their jobs and to give your best effort daily. Our company is like a sports team and we should work together and help each other win. The last thing that I want to do is fire someone because most of us have families. Even if you don't, your bills still have to be paid and you have to support yourself. Let's be productive and thanks for your attention and y' all have ten minutes to finish your meals", Lucas said.

The rest of the workday goes well and the employees are productive and in much better spirits. Later that night, Lucas and Shelia are lying in bed and he shares his thoughts of the day with her.

"Shelia, I know that I did the right thing in firing those racist workers, but it still leaves a bad taste in my mouth", Lucas said, disturbed.

"Lucas, you did what was necessary and you shouldn't feel bad about it", Shelia said, massaging his shoulders.

"I know, but it never feels good to fire someone."

"Those bigots deserved to be fired and I'm happy that you dumped their asses. Lucas, I've been wanting to tell you something for a while now, but I've been holding back until now", Shelia said, looking into his eyes.

"What is it Shelia?", Lucas asked, frowning.

"I've been having an uncomfortable feeling about you working in Butlerville. Maybe you should consider working somewhere else."

"Shelia, I appreciate your concern, but I'm not going to let a couple of racist nut jobs drive me out of Butlerville."

"I'm just concerned about your safety."

"I understand Shelia, but your husband is going to be fine. I know self-defense pretty well and if someone tries to mess with me or my family, they're going to regret it."

"I know that you can defend yourself Lucas and I'm just concerned. I love you and I don't know what our family would do without you."

"Shelia, stop talking like that and stop worrying. I'm not going anywhere", Lucas said.

"Okay, I'll try", Shelia promised.

"Don't try; just do it."

"Okay."

Thirty minutes later, they both fall asleep and the next morning, Lucas wakes up groggy and for some reason, not well rested. He dreads having to go into work and wishes that he could stay home, but knows that it's not a good option. Lucas gets out of the bed slowly and Shelia is still sleeping soundly and occasionally snoring. He makes his way toward the bathroom to freshen up his body and when he's finished, he walks out of the bathroom and he begins to hear a soft voice telling him, TAKE YOUR GUN TO WORK WITH YOU. Lucas is puzzled by the voice and he tries to shake off the voice and focuses on what he's going to fix himself for breakfast. Lucas is up earlier than usual and he decides to cook himself an egg and sausage sandwich and a couple of pancakes and he decides to have some orange juice to wash down his food. Before he starts eating, Lucas says a prayer of thanks to God and then enjoys his breakfast. When he's finished, Lucas places his eating utensils in the kitchen sink and then rips off a couple of pieces of paper towel off a roll and cleans his mouth and hands. Once again, he hears the same soft voice speaking to him, saying, TAKE YOUR GUN TO WORK WITH YOU, and Lucas tries to ignore the voice, but can't completely. He finishes getting ready for work and before he leaves the house, Lucas gets on his knees and reaches under their bed for a shoe box which contains his gun and gun holster. He leaves the house and it turns out to be a typical work day and when Lucas gets off work, he decides to stop off at the BP gas station to fill up his gas tank. While he's driving toward the station, he hears that familiar voice telling him, BEFORE YOU GET OUT OF YOUR CAR, TAKE YOUR GUN WITH YOU. Lucas feels anxious and uncomfortable and when he arrives at the gas station, he takes the gun and gun holster out and places the gun on the side of his holster before walking into the station. After paying for his gas, Lucas walks out and begins filling up his tank. When he's finished, he's about to get back into his car when he's suddenly approached by a menacing young white man. He's holding a huge butcher knife and the young white man is pointing it directly toward Lucas. He has an angry, no-nonsense look on his face and he yells at Lucas.

"Give me your keys and your money old man! You know what this is and hurry up!", he demanded.

"Okay! Okay! I'll give you my wallet and I don't want any trouble!", Lucas said.

"Hurry up before I hurt you!"

"Okay! I'll give you whatever you want!"

Lucas reaches toward his gun holster, pretending to be pulling out his wallet. While Lucas is doing this, he also keeps his eyes glued to the young man. He believes that Lucas is taking too long in handing over the items and he lunges at Lucas with his knife. As the young man tries to stab Lucas, he fires off a couple of bullets, hitting the attempted carjacker. He's shocked and then he realizes that he's been shot and discovers himself bleeding. The young man holds his right side and limps away as fast as possible like a wounded puppy. Moments later, Lucas gets into his car and speeds off and thanks God for sparing his life. Two weeks later, Lucas and Shelia have arrived home not long after they have gone grocery shopping when the phone rings. Lucas goes to answer it and he sees on the Caller ID that Mayor Lane's number is appearing and Lucas answers it.

"Hello Mayor Lane. How are you and your family?", Lucas asked.

"We're alright Lucas. How is your family? How is your job coming along?", Mayor Lane asked.

"My family is fine and the job is coming along fine. Early on, I had a few road bumps but things are going smoothly now."

"Well, sometimes, it takes a little time to get settled in at a new job. I'm happy that things are going well for you."

"Mayor Lane, I want to thank you for putting in some good words for me at B. Mitchell. I really appreciate it and I don't know if I would've been offered the job if it wasn't for you."

"You're giving me too much credit Lucas. Your resume stood on its own and you would've received the position anyway", Mayor Lane said, confidently.

"I don't know about that, but I'll never forget what you did", Lucas said, thankfully.

"No problem. Lucas, I called to ask you something."

"What is it Mayor?"

"I would like to invite you and your family over for dinner."

"Wow! Mr. Mayor, I'm so honored."

"Lucas, if you and Shelia don't have other plans, we would love to have y' all over tomorrow evening. We usually start eating dinner at about six o' clock and we'll have plenty of food", Mayor Lane assured him.

"Mayor Lane, I would love to come over. Let me check to see if Shelia has something that she wants to do."

"Understood. And by the way Lucas, I'll send a limo to pick up your family and take you back home. My limo driver's name is Paul and it will be the Wilson Limousine Company. Your family can come over here and enjoy some good food and have a good time."

"Hold on a minute Mr. Mayor and I'll get right back with you", Lucas said.

"Alright", Mayor Lane said.

Lucas gets off the phone and looks toward Shelia and asks her if she wants to do something special the following evening. She says no and then asks Lucas why he asked her that and Lucas tells her about the Mayor's invitation. Shelia is thrilled and agrees that they should accept the Mayor's dinner invitation. Lucas smiles and then resumes talking to Mayor Lane.

"Mayor Lane, we'll be over tomorrow for dinner", Lucas said.

"Great and we look forward to seeing y' all! We're going to have pork chops, beef stew, cornbread, and collard greens. And we're going to have sodas and Kool-Aid to go along with the food! Make sure that y' all bring your appetites!", Mayor Lane said, excitedly.

"I'm getting hungry just thinking about all that food", Lucas joked.

"And Lucas, your limo will arrive at about five-thirty, give or take some minutes. Just be alert", Mayor Lane said.

"We will Mr. Mayor."

"We'll see y' all tomorrow evening. Lucas, and y' all have a great evening and good-bye."

"Good-bye Mr. Mayor and your family do the same."

The following evening, Lucas and his family are in the limo and on their way to the Mayor's Residence. Chester and Melvin are in awe of the limo.

"This is pretty cool and a limo is a million times better than a taxi", Chester said.

"It's so roomy and comfortable and I could see myself sleeping in something like this", Melvin said.

"Chester, if you make it to the NBA, this will be standard procedure", Lucas said.

"Well Dad, I have to concentrate on playing College Basketball first."

"I know, but there's nothing wrong with thinking about something like that."

"I could get used to nice things like this", Shelia said, smiling.

"Family, let's get back grounded in reality and enjoy this ride for what it is", Lucas said.

"You're right. Paul, do you know how much longer it will be before we arrive at the Mayor's Residence?", Shelia asked.

"We should be pulling up at their home any minute now", Paul said.

Minutes later, they arrive and they're walking into the Mayor's Residence. The mayor and his wife Karen greet them and they also introduce their two teenage sons Kevin and Mark to Chester and Melvin. Mayor Lane encourages them to have a seat on their living room sofa and make they graciously accept his offer and sit down. The mayor indicates that the food is almost ready.

"I'm sorry that everything isn't ready. I had to make a trip to the grocery store and buy some important ingredients", Mayor Lane said.

"Don't worry about that Mayor Lane. We're so honored that you and your wife invited us and the limo that you sent us was so nice", Lucas said.

"I'm happy that your family enjoyed it."

"Mayor Lane, your home is so beautiful", Shelia said, looking around.

"Thank you, Shelia, but I have to give most of the credit to Karen for that. She's done a great job of decorating our home with antiques and plants", Mayor Lane said, smiling at her.

"That's very kind of you Dugan and Shelia, I have a real passion for collecting antiques and plants. Every year, during the Spring, in Butlerville, we host the National Antiques Collectors Showcase. Dealers and Collectors from all over the United States come here and I always look forward to it!", Karen said.

"It's a beautiful thing when you discover something that you love."

"It sure is. Shelia, do you collect antiques and plants too Shelia?"

"Well, not so much antiques, but every year I plant a garden."

"You do? What do you like to plant?", Karen asked, fascinated.

"Tomatoes, squash, kale, or whatever else that I'm in the mood to plant", Shelia said.

"That's great and there's nothing like some good old school food."

"I agree."

"Mayor Lane, I'm looking at your wall and I see that you're a baseball fan", Lucas observed.

"You're right and I love Major League Baseball. I'm a huge Chicago Cubs fan and that picture is with Mark Grace and I was a big fan of his. Karen and I were attending a Cubs game and they had a bobblehead promotion of him. Some friends of mine used to work for the Cubs and they introduced us. I loved his sweet swing and he's a good guy too", Mayor Lane said.

"I'm a baseball fan too Mayor Lane. We're rivals because I'm a Chicago White Sox fan and my all-time favorite player is Harold Baines. He was so consistently good and I still don't believe that some baseball fans realize just how good he really was."

"He was damn good Lucas. I'm a National League man and you're an American League man, but we share a love of baseball."

"Great point Mayor."

"Everyone, the food is ready and it's time to load your plates", Karen yelled from the kitchen.

Mayor Lane escorts everyone into the kitchen and everyone fixes their plates and pour up their beverage of choice. When everyone has finished fixing their plates, they sit down at a rectangular table. Before everyone begins eating, Mayor Lane leads everyone in prayer and when he's finished, the mayor addresses the group.

"We don't want anyone to be shy about eating this food because we have plenty", Mayor Lane assured them.

"The food looks and smells so good", Shelia said.

"Thank you", Karen said.

"You're welcome."

"Lucas, our sons have a couple of things in common", Mayor Lane said.

"We do?", Chester asked, puzzled.

"Our oldest son Mark is a shooting guard on the Butlerville High School basketball team. Last year, Mark set the school record for the most points in a game."

"Are you serious?"

"Yes, and we're so proud of him. And my alma mater, the University of Illinois at Champaign has shown strong interest in him. It would be nice to have Mark play there, but I want him to make the best decision for himself."

"We can relate to that. We were telling this to Chester before he signed with Bradley University", Lucas said.

"Bradley is a very good University."

"Dad, I scored all those points but we still lost the game. A victory would've been much better.", Mark said.

"I can relate to that Mark. Our high school didn't win as many games as I would've liked", Chester said, nodding his head.

"Losing stinks and it's all about winning."

"I agree."

"Chester, do you want to play basketball in our backyard after dinner?", Mark said.

"I would love to", Chester said.

"Alright."

"I'm the captain of the Butlerville Debate Team and we won the Regional Championship last year", Kevin said, proudly.

"And I'm the captain of the Center City Debate Team and we won the Conference Championship", Melvin said.

"Isn't that a real coincidence? They're both captains of their debate teams and what are the odds of that?", Lucas asked.

"We have some very accomplished children", Karen said.

"Melvin, do you play chess?", Kevin asked.

"I've never played it before", Melvin said.

"Would you like to learn?"

"Sure."

"Well, we can hang out in my room after dinner and I'll teach you the game."

"Alright."

After dinner, the adults continue their conversations while the boys are enjoying their activities. Two hours later, Lucas and Shelia thank Mayor Lane and Karen for dinner and their hospitality. They encourage Lucas and Shelia to stay in touch and they promise to do so. Moments later, Paul shows up in the limo and takes them back home.

Chapter Four

Bittersweet Offer

Lucas is outside in the yard cutting their grass and it's a scorching hot July afternoon. He occasionally wipes his forehead in an effort to fight off the sweat and keep it out of his eyes. When he's finished, Shelia comes out of the house and brings him a plastic bottle of Gatorade. She compliments Lucas on the condition of the grass.

"Lucas, you did an outstanding job cutting the grass. I believe that it's the best-looking grass in the neighborhood", Shelia said.

"Thanks Shelia", Lucas said, accepting the Gatorade.

"No problem."

"It's so hot out here and it feels like my hair is on fire", Lucas joked.

"Well, I hope that the Gatorade cools it off", Shelia said, laughing.

At that point, their neighbor Gloria Jones from across the street comes out of her house. She opens her mailbox and takes a couple of documents out of it. Gloria glances across the street and sees Lucas and Shelia. She waves and speaks to them.

"Lucas and Shelia, how are y' all doing?", Gloria asked.

"We're fine and how are y' all?", Shelia asked.

"It's too hot isn't it?"

"Too hot", Lucas said, wiping his forehead.

"Make sure that y' all drink plenty of liquids because you can easily pass out in weather like this", Gloria warned.

"We'll be sure to do that Gloria and thank you for your concern."

"You're welcome and y' all have a great rest of the day", Gloria said.

"Right back at you", Shelia said.

Gloria goes back into her house and closes the door behind her and Lucas and Shelia resume their earlier conversation.

"Lucas, maybe you should stop working for the day because you've done a lot", Shelia said, concerned.

"No Shelia, I want to trim our hedges now and I might as well do everything", Lucas said, waving her off.

"Are you sure?"

"Yes I am and besides, tomorrow is Sunday and I can rest and relax all day."

"Okay."

"Shelia, I'm going to be alright and I don't believe that it's going to take as long as you think."

"Well, I'll be in the house if you need me", Shelia said.

"Alright", Lucas said.

Shelia goes into the house and Lucas opens his Gatorade bottle and drinks all of it. He then throws his bottle into their recycling bin and then begins trimming the hedges. Almost an hour later, Shelia comes out of the house with garbage bags, a broom, and a dustpan. Lucas sees Shelia and asks her what she's doing.

"I'm helping my loving husband", Shelia said.

"Shelia, I told you that I would let you know if I needed your help. I have everything under control and I---

"I'm not arguing with you Lucas. I'm helping you and that's the end of the discussion."

"Well, I'm not going to argue with you beautiful lady", Lucas said, pointing at Shelia.

"Oh Lucas", Shelia said, blushing.

"What were you going to do?", Lucas asked.

"I'm going to sweep our sidewalk and pick up some hedge pieces. And then, I'm going to put them in some garbage bags and place them in our garbage can. I'm going to help you with whatever you need", Shelia said.

"That's so sweet of you Shelia and I appreciate that."

"No problem Lucas."

Lucas finishes trimming the hedges while Shelia sweeps and gathers hedge pieces and other debris from the sidewalk and their yard. She places the debris into a couple of garbage bags and a short time later, Lucas finishes his work. Shelia goes into the house and Lucas pushes his lawnmower toward their garage to put up. As he's doing so, Lucas hears his neighbor Earl Jackson calling him and he stops and turns around.

"Earl, how are you doing? I haven't seen you in a while and it's good to see you", Lucas said, as Earl is approaching him.

"Same here Lucas. I've been working a lot of overtime at my job and it's been kicking my butt", Earl said.

"I can relate to do that."

"Lucas, I came over to ask if you had some extra gasoline that you can spare. The gas in my lawnmower is low and I don't know If it will be enough to cut all my grass."

"You can use some of mine and you can walk with me to the garage."

"Thank you Lucas and I would be willing to give you a couple of dollars."

"Nonsense Earl. You've helped me out like this and we're neighbors."

"I appreciate that Lucas."

"You're welcome Earl and is your family alright?", Lucas asked.

"We're okay. My wife Lisa is three months pregnant and this will be our second child", Earl said, proudly.

"Congratulations! That's a blessing!"

"Thank you Lucas."

"When you see Lisa, tell her that we said congratulations."

"I will and Lucas, is everything alright with your family?", Earl asked.

"We're fine. I'm a supervisor at the B. Mitchell Candy Company in Butlerville", Lucas said.

"That's great and how long have you been there?"

"About two months now."

"I'm happy for you and B. Mitchell has some good candy. I love their candy bars with peanuts."

"Yeah, our candies are pretty good."

"You and Shelia have always been hard working people."

"We do what we can. Earl, how much gasoline do you think that you'll need?", Lucas asked.

"About a cup or two if you can spare it", Earl said.

"No problem, just hold up your cup and I'll begin pouring."

"Alright."

Earl holds up his cup and Lucas cautiously pours two cups of gasoline into it and afterward, Earl thanks Lucas. They shake hands and Earl walks toward home and Lucas locks the garage door. He goes into the house and freshens up his body and change his clothes. When Lucas is finished, he joins Shelia in the bedroom and they place themselves near their air conditioner. They enjoy the refreshing cool air and each other while watching their favorite television shows. The rest of the day is uneventful and a week later, Lucas and Shelia are watching television on a Saturday afternoon. They're in the living room waiting on Shelia's parents to show up. Shelia is excited and indicates this to Lucas.

"Lucas, it has been a while since we've seen my parents. I can't wait until they get here", Shelia said, with sparkles in her eyes.

"I know and I always looking forward to seeing your parents. What time did you say that they're supposed to be here?", Lucas asked, smiling.

"About two o' clock. They should be in here in about another fifteen minutes", Shelia said, looking down at her watch.

"Good", Lucas said.

Lucas and Shelia continue talking and watching television for another twenty minutes. Then they hear the doorbell ring and Shelia gets up from the sofa and goes to answer it. Her parents, Albert and Wendy Lawson are outside the door and Shelia opens the door and lets them in. They all greet each other warmly and share hugs and kisses. Wendy gives Shelia a couple of sweet potato pies covered with aluminum foil and Shelia is pleasantly surprised. She thanks her mom and a short time later, they enter the living room and Lucas hugs Wendy and gives Albert a firm handshake. Lucas and Shelia encourage them to sit down and make themselves feel at home. They do so and Sheila asks them if they want something to drink. Wendy and Albert thank Shelia for her offer and they decline. Moments later, Shelia asks them how they've been.

"We've been fine. I've been doing housework and visiting friends. I've been retired from my job at the Variety Spice Company for almost a year now. I am really enjoying my retirement', Wendy said.

"And early next year, I'm going to join your mother in retirement", Albert said.

"Dad, you're going to retire?", Shelia asked, surprised.

"Yes Shelia, I'm going to retire from the Jackson Clayton Foundry. I've been working there for thirty years now and my body is starting to wear down."

"Dad, you've always been an energetic person. I thought that you were going to work there longer."

"Well, Shelia, your father is getting older. And being a welder is hard, grueling work, although I love it. One day I woke up and decided that I didn't want to do it anymore. Besides, God has been great to us and your mother and I are financially comfortable."

"Mr. And Miss Lawson, I admire your work ethic. I pray that y' all have a great retirement", Lucas said.

"Thank you Lucas and we appreciate your kind words", Albert said.

"I'm looking forward to spending retirement with Albert. We're going to have so much fun!", Wendy said, winking at Albert.

"We sure are Wendy", Albert said, looking deeply into her eyes.

"I pray that Shelia and I will always have a strong marriage like y' all do", Lucas said, smiling.

"I have no doubt that y' all will. As long as both of you are always willing to work hard to keep your marriage strong, it will last", Wendy said, confidently.

"You're not going to always like each other. But as long as your love and respect remain for each other, your marriage will last", Albert said.

"I agree."

"Mom, thank you again for bringing over your famous sweet potato pies. They brought back some great childhood memories", Shelia said.

"I don't know about the famous part Shelia, but I thank you for the compliment. I was in a cooking mood, so I decided to fix them", Wendy said.

"The kids in the neighborhood loved your pies too."

"I remember and those were good days. Lucas, I don't want you and the boys to be shy about eating these pies."

"Thank you. I promise you that your pies won't go to waste. We love sweet potato pies too", Lucas said.

"Alright."

"How are Chester and Melvin?", Albert asked.

"They're doing well", Lucas said.

"This is a wonderful family gathering", Shelia said, smiling.

"It sure is", Lucas agreed.

They all continue their conversation for another hour and then Wendy and Arthur indicate to Lucas and Shelia that they're getting ready to leave. Everyone gets up and exchange kisses and hugs and agree to stay in touch more. A short time later, Wendy and Arthur leave and the rest of the day is uneventful. A week later, Lucas and Shelia are at home relaxing on the living room sofa. They're enjoying each other's company and during their conversation, Lucas comments on Shelia's hair.

"Shelia, I know that you've been wanting to get your hair done, "Lucas said.

"Yeah, and I want to get this nappy hair together. I've been so busy lately that I haven't had the time", Shelia said.

"When do you think that you might go to the Beauty Salon?"

"I don't know, but why are you asking? "Does it look that bad?", Shelia asked, massaging her hair.

"No Shelia. This is for you when you decide to go", Lucas said, pulling out a one-hundred bill out of his pants pocket.

Shelia is surprised and is speechless.

"I just want you to treat yourself Shelia. Just take this Shelia", Lucas said, giving her the money. Shelia accepts it and her eyes widen with joy and then she thanks and kisses Lucas for what seems like an eternity. A short time later, Lucas speaks to Shelia.

"Shelia Lightfoot, I love you very much and you're my beautiful black queen. You're a damn good woman and you deserve this", Lucas said, staring lovingly into her eyes.

"Lucas Lightfoot, I love you very much too and you're my handsome black king. You're a damn good man and our family is blessed to have you, Shelia said, wiping away a tear.

"It's all true."

"I'll definitely go to Monique's Beauty Salon now. This weekend would be great because I don't have to work. I'll probably call them later and schedule an appointment, preferably during the afternoon."

"Whatever works for you Shelia."

"Thanks again Lucas", Shelia said, kissing him.

"No problem Shelia", Lucas said, returning a kiss.

Later the day, Shelia calls Monique to schedule an appointment. Monique asks Shelia if a three o' clock appointment would be good for her. Shelia assures her that it is and then Shelia asks Monique if she can come in Saturday. and Monique tells her yes and then Monique asks Shelia what type of hairstyle that she wants.

"I want something that looks good and is easy to manage. I'm tired of my hair looking a hot mess", Shelia said.

"I understand. Shelia. I think that you should consider getting some Faux Locs or maybe some dreadlocks. They're versatile and you can do a lot of experimenting with them", Monique suggested.

"That sounds good and what else would you suggest?"

"I think that twisted braids would also look good on you Shelia. They would fit your face and I've noticed that more young women are getting them."

"Really?"

"Yes, especially young professional black women."

"That's interesting. You can hook me up with the twisted braids and I want to look glamorous for my husband. This hairstyle will make me look younger and he's a good-looking man. I know that women check him out, especially younger ones. I always want to be the one for him", Shelia said.

"I can totally relate to that because I feel that way about my husband. Do you want any more hairstyle questions Shelia?", Monique asked.

"No Monique. I'm going to get the twisted braids because they sound perfect for me."

"Okay Shelia, twisted braids it will be."

"How much will this cost Monique?", Shelia asked.

"Sixty dollars."

"That's reasonable."

"Shelia, do you have any other questions?", Monique asked.

"No and I'll see you at three o' clock on Saturday", Shelia said.

"See you then Shelia. Good-bye."

"Good-bye Monique."

Later that evening, Shelia enters the house and Lucas is amazed when he sees her new hairstyle.

"Well look at you Shelia! You look so beautiful and smoking hot! Monique really hooked you up! Wow!", Lucas said.

"Thank you Lucas and I'm happy that you love my new look", Shelia said.

"I sure do and you should rock that hairstyle for a while. I absolutely love it!"

"Well, since you like it so much, I'll do just that. Does it make me look younger?"

Lucas is caught off guard by Shelia's question and he pauses before answering her question. He carefully studies her face and braids, and indeed, Shelia does look younger. Lucas has an even greater appreciation of how beautiful Shelia is and he has a flashback to their wedding day. He reflects on some of their great memories, not only as husband and wife, but also as parents. He smiles and then snaps out of his reflective state and answers Shelia's question.

"Shelia, it does make you look younger and you're as beautiful as ever", Lucas said.

"Thank you, Lucas and that means so much to me. And thank you for treating me to a new look", Shelia said.

"You're welcome, Shelia. That glow on your beautiful face makes it all worthwhile."

"I feel like a new woman!"

"I'm glad Shelia! I cooked dinner and we have pork chops, rice and gravy, string beans. And there's a two-liter of Pepsi in the refrigerator. All of the food is still on the stove", Lucas said.

"I appreciate that Lucas and this is right on time because I'm hungry! I can't wait to dig in", Shelia said, smacking her lips.

"Help yourself sweetheart."

"I'm going to do just that."

"And I'm going to join you Shelia."

Minutes later, Lucas and Shelia fix their plates and then sit down at the kitchen table. After they finish praying, they conversate and talk about various topics. When they're finished eating, they wash up their dishes and decide to relax and watch television in their bedroom. The rest of the day is uneventful and three months later, Mayor Lane has invited Lucas to visit him in his office. The mayor urges Lucas to sit down in a chair in front of his desk and Lucas sits down. Then the mayor speaks.

"Lucas, I'm glad that you could make it", Mayor Lane said, grimly.

"No problem Mayor. I don't like your facial expression and is there something wrong?", Lucas asked, concerned.

"Well, these are not the best of times for me."

"Are you worried about winning re-election? You're a popular mayor in Butlerville and you should win re-election easily."

"Lucas, I've been in politics for a long time now. I don't take anything for granted and I've seen little known candidates defeat incumbents. I also remember losing in high school when I ran for class president", Mayor Lane said.

"But this isn't high school Mayor Lane. I don't believe that you have anything to worry about and the. residents of Butlerville love you", Lucas assured him.

"Well, the results of my re-election campaign probably won't matter."

"Mayor Lane, what is wrong and why would you say something like that?"

"I went to my doctor recently for my routine checkup."

"What did your doctor tell you?", Lucas asked.

"She told me that I had Lou Gehring's Disease, also known as ALS", Mayor Lane said, letting out a long sigh.

"Mr. Mayor, I'm so sorry to hear this. What can our family do for you? Do you need anything?"

"I appreciate your concern Lucas and I'm okay for now."

"As a baseball fan, I've heard of this disease and I know that it affects a person's neurological functions", Lucas said.

"Correct Lucas and it affects the nerve and brain cells."

"How?"

"As this disease progresses, your muscles become malnourished and your brain gradually loses its ability to control your bodily functions. Every day activities become a challenge, such as eating and speaking. In other words, you lose your ability to live independently."

"Mayor Lane, is there anything that can be done to improve your health?", Lucas asked, hopeful.

"Unfortunately, Lucas, there is no cure for ALS. The typical ALS patient lives for about three to five years after being diagnosed. My doctor suggested that I perform stretching exercises daily because they can increase my blood circulation. And she also prescribed the drug Riluzole and urged me to eat a healthy, balanced diet", Mayor Lane said.

"This is such a shock and this was the last thing that I was expecting to hear."

"Lucas, even if I am re-elected, I'm probably not going to live out my four-year term. If I die before then, Nate Greenburg would automatically become the Interim Mayor. He's the longest serving member of the Butlerville City Council and he would serve out the remainder of my term. And then a special election would be held to elect the next Mayor."

"I don't like hearing you talk like this Mr. Mayor."

"I can imagine how you feel Lucas, but I'm not going to sugar coat this. I'm dying and it's just a matter of when the good Lord is ready for me."

"Don't say that because you're still here and there's always hope."

"I know Lucas, but I'm also being realistic. I'm going to cherish and appreciate every day that I have left on this earth. I'm going to enjoy my family and friends and the residents of Butlerville as much as possible", Mayor Lane said.

"I admire your attitude Mr. Mayor", Lucas said.

"Lucas, I've accepted my fate and I'm nobody special. We all have to face death eventually."

"I know."

"And I'm going to make sure that my business affairs are in order. I don't want my family to have problems when I'm gone. I'm also going to talk to my financial planner about my investments and make sure that my finances are in order."

"Have you told your family yet?", Lucas asked.

"Yes I did, and as you can imagine, they were shocked and devastated. Karen cried so much that it scared me and I thought that I was going to have to take her to the hospital. Sharing that news was the most difficult thing that I've ever done", Mayor Lane said, wiping away a squirting tear from his eye.

"We'll be praying for you and your family Mayor Lane", Lucas said, patting the Mayor on his shoulder.

"Thank you Lucas and you'll never know how much your friendship means to me."

"Right back at you Mr. Mayor."

"And because you've been such a great friend Lucas, I want to ask you to do me a favor", Mayor Lane asked.

"What is it?", Lucas asked.

"When I'm gone, I want you to run for Mayor of Butlerville."

"Me? I'm honored that you have such a high opinion of me Mayor Lane. But I don't have any political experience."

"Lucas, there is a first time for everything. May I remind you that President Trump didn't have any political experience either?"

"You make a good point. And may I remind you that I'm a black man? Butlerville Is a white town and I don't know if the residents would elect a black man to be its mayor", Lucas said, doubtful.

"You're really a black man Lucas? I never noticed that before", Mayor Lane joked.

They both burst out laughing for a couple of minutes and when they calm down, the Mayor resumes talking.

"Lucas, what does that have to do with anything? We have a lot of good people living in Butlerville and I believe that you underestimate the good will in this town. I wouldn't give a damn if you were purple Lucas and you're a good man. I love Butlerville and I want the town to be in good hands when I'm gone."

"What about Nate Greenburg? Don't you think that he would be a good Mayor?"

"Nate Greenburg has had some ethics violations and a disorderly conduct charge in his past."

"Maybe he's changed", Lucas reasoned.

"That's possible, but I wouldn't bet any money on that", Mayor Lane said, unconvinced.

"I don't know Mayor Lane. I ---

"It would give me a piece of mind knowing that you would be holding the keys to Butlerville. My political instincts tell me that you would do a great job."

"Mr. Mayor, I now understand why the people in this town continue to re-elect you."

"What do you now understand?", Mayor Lane asked, intrigued.

"You're a great salesman and you're doing a great sales job on me", Lucas admitted.

"Thank you, Lucas. Sometimes I have to use that skill to help me get legislation passed."

"I'll talk this over with Shelia and then get in touch with you", Lucas promised.

"That's fine with me Lucas. Family is the most important thing and take all the time you need to make a decision", Mayor Lane cautioned.

"Okay. Well Mr. Mayor, I'm going to leave now and if you need anything, don't hesitate to call."

"Thank you Lucas and I'll keep that in mind. Have a good evening Lucas and good-bye."

"You too Mayor Lane and good-bye."

Later that night, Lucas and Shelia are lying in bed watching television. Lucas is quieter than usual and has barely spoken. Shelia is concerned and asks him if there's something wrong.

"Yes there is Shelia", Lucas said.

"What is it?", Shelia asked.

"I visited Mayor Lane's office today and he shared some terrible news with me."

"What was it?"

"He told me that he was diagnosed with Lou Gehring's Disease, or ALS."

"What? That's horrible and I feel badly for him and his family. I've heard of ALS, but what is it exactly?", Shelia asked.

"It's a degenerative neurological disease that eventually robs someone of their ability to move around freely. Being able to perform basic things such as walking, talking, or eating become difficult. And eventually, ALS patients can't take care of themselves. The disease was named after the late Lou Gehring and he's a Major League

Baseball Hall of Famer that played for the New York Yankees", Lucas said.

"Thanks for educating me Lucas."

"The mayor also asked me for a favor and I told him that I would discuss it with you."

"What did he ask you?", Shelia asked.

"If he dies, Mayor Lane asked me to run for Mayor of Butlerville", Lucas said.

"Really?"

"Yes and I've never really thought of myself as a political person. Mayor Lane thinks that I would do a good job and I wanted to know what you thought about this."

"Wow. The mayor has a very high opinion of you Lucas. Well, you've been a supervisor for many years and you're a natural leader and an honest, honorable man. I wish that more elected officials had your qualities."

"Shelia, hearing you say good things like that brings warm feelings to my heart."

"Well, it's the truth. Lucas, if you decided to run for Mayor, I would totally support you", Shelia promised.

"I appreciate that Shelia and I feel somewhat guilty about this conversation. Mayor Lane is dying and I don't want to believe it. This conversation feels selfish because he's still with us", Lucas said.

"Well, Lucas, he did want you to discuss this with me, but I understand what you mean. The mayor is a strong man and he will fight this disease with everything that he can."

"He's definitely a fighter", Lucas said.

"Yes he is", Shelia agreed.

"I wonder what Chester and Melvin would think about their father running for Mayor."

"They would be proud and supportive. For now, we'll pray and help the Mayor in any way that we can."

"I told the Mayor the same thing."

"We're on the same page."

"Yes we are."

They continue conversating and watching television for another hour before going to sleep and then Lucas and Shelia decide to go to sleep. A week later, Lucas is driving home from his work day and when he arrives in Center City, he decides to stop at the Citgo Gas Station to fill up his tank. Lucas goes into the station and to his pleasant surprise, he sees his former employee Evelyn Hampton at Martha's Cheese Factory. Lucas calls her name and she looks around and spots him and her face breaks out into a huge smile. Evelyn walks toward Lucas and they exchange hugs and he asks her how she's been.

"I'm doing great Lucas and what about you?", Evelyn asked.

"I'm doing fine Evelyn. Are you working right now?", Lucas asked.

"I sure am. When Martha's went out of business, it only took me a little more than a month to get another job. I'm working at the Davenport Paper Company in Jackson."

"I'm so happy for you Evelyn. You were always one of my favorite employees and you worked hard and never gave me problems."

"Thank you for the kind words, Lucas and you made things easier as a supervisor. I'll never forget the compassion that you had for me when my father died. You're the best supervisor that I've ever worked for."

"Thank you Evelyn and I know what it's like to lose someone close to you. I remember the emotions that I felt when my brother died and he was also my best friend", Lucas said.

"Losing a loved one is tough", Evelyn said.

"It sure is."

"Lucas, are you working now?"

"I landed on my feet with another job too. I'm the supervisor at the B. Mitchell Candy Company in Butlerville and God is great."

"Yes, he is and I'm happy for you Lucas."

"I'm happy for you too Evelyn."

"Well Lucas, I have to get home and start up dinner. It was great to see you", Evelyn said, smiling.

"Same here Evelyn and you take care", Lucas said, smiling back at her.

"You too Lucas."

Evelyn walks out of the gas station and Lucas walks toward the cashier to purchase his gas. To his surprise, he's the only one in there and he pays him ten dollars and then walks out. Lucas fills his gas tank and minutes later, he heads home. Two weeks later, Lucas and Shelia are sitting in the living room and they're discussing inviting Mayor Lane and Karen over for dinner.

"Shelia, I think it's only fair that we invite Mayor Lane and Karen over. We had a great time at the Mayor's residence and I think that we should return the favor", Lucas said.

"I agree Lucas and I think that this upcoming weekend would be a good time. We don't have to work this weekend", Shelia said.

"Shelia, what foods do you think that we should cook?"

Shelia pauses for a moment and then answers Lucas' question.

"Well, maybe some pork chops smothered with rice and gravy, macaroni and cheese and meatloaf. What suggestions do you have Lucas?", Shelia asked.

"I think that we could also have some string beans or some glory greens. And naturally, we need something to drink", Lucas said.

"What beverages do you have in mind Lucas?"

"I don't know if Mayor Lane and Karen drink alcohol. I think that some beer would be nice and I'll ask Mayor Lane if they drink alcohol. If they do, I'll pick up some beer."

"Beer would be fine with me", Shelia said.

"I'm going to call the mayor right now and invite them over", Lucas said, walking toward the phone.

"Okay."

Moments later, Lucas dials the mayor's number. The phone rings three times before Mayor Lane answers it in a pleasant voice.

"Hello", Mayor Lane said.

"Hello Mayor Lane, this is Lucas and, how are you?", Lucas asked.

"Lucas, it's great hearing from you. How is everything going with you?", Mayor Lane asked.

"I'm fine and the family is too."

"Same here Lucas."

"Mayor Lane, I called you for a specific reason."

"What is it Lucas?"

"Shelia and I wanted to invite you and Karen over for dinner this upcoming Saturday evening. Would y' all be able to make it?", Lucas asked.

"That is so nice of you and Shelia. Hold on a moment Lucas and let me ask Karen something", Mayor Lane said.

"Okay."

Mayor Lane puts Lucas on hold for a couple of minutes before resuming his conversation with Lucas.

"Lucas, we would love to come over for dinner. What time should we arrive?"

"Hold on Mayor Lane while I ask Shelia."

"Okay."

Lucas puts Mayor Lane on hold briefly and moments later, Lucas resumes talking to the Mayor.

"Mayor, you and Karen should arrive at six, maybe seven o' clock."

"How does six-thirty sound Lucas?"

"Sounds good to me Mayor Lane. I need to ask you another question."

"What is it?"

"Do you and Karen drink alcohol?"

"Occasionally. Why?"

"We were thinking about having beer with dinner. We didn't know whether or not you and Karen drank alcohol."

"Beer is okay with us Lucas."

"Is there a favorite beer that y' all like?", Lucas asked.

"We usually drink Miller Genuine Draft or Miller Lite", Mayor Lane said.

"I'll buy some Miller Genuine Draft. Mayor Lane, Shelia and I look forward to seeing you and Karen."

"We look forward to seeing you and Shelia. Thank you for inviting us", Mayor Lane said.

"You're welcome, Mayor and we'll see you and Karen then. Good-bye Mayor."

"Good-bye Lucas."

Lucas hangs up. A couple of hours later, he's in the kitchen pouring himself a glass of milk when he hears Shelia calling him.

"Lucas! Lucas!", Shelia yelled.

"What is it?!", Lucas asked.

"It's the telephone for you."

"Who is it?"

"It's your cousin Hakim."

"Okay, I'll be right there."

Lucas puts the gallon of milk back in the refrigerator and picks up his cup from the kitchen cabinet. Moments later, he walks into the living room and Shelia gives Lucas the phone and he says hello.

"Lucas, how is my favorite cousin doing?", Hakim asked.

"I'm fine and what about you?", Lucas asked, frowning.

"I could be better."

"How? What's wrong?", Lucas asked, suspiciously.

"Lucas, I could use fifty dollars", Hakim said.

"I could use fifty dollars too Hakim", Lucas said sarcastically.

"So now you have jokes", Hakim said.

"Why do you need fifty dollars?"

"I'm having money problems and I wanted to know if you would help me out."

"What type of money problems?"

"Come on Lucas, why are you sweating me about this?"

"Because I loaned you two hundred dollars Hakim and you never paid me back. You promised me that you would pay me back when you received your income taxes. A man's word is supposed to be his bond."

"Things happen Lucas and you know how it is. So, favorite cousin, are you going to loan me fifty dollars?", Hakim asked.

"Something always seems to happen to you Hakim. Have you lost your mind? You still haven't paid me back and you have the nerve to ask me for more money? Are you serious?", Lucas asked, raising his voice.

"We're family Lucas. I---

"I don't give a damn about that Hakim! Family is family and business is business!"

"I can't believe that you're not going to help me out Lucas."

"I'll never loan you another penny!"

"Lucas I---

"Good-bye Hakim!"

Lucas hangs up and he's steaming angry and he takes a couple of deep breaths in an effort to calm himself down. A short time later, Lucas has calmed down and gathered his thoughts. Then he begins speaking to Shelia.

"Shelia, he has a lot of nerve and he's been a user of people all his life. I should've known better and my instincts told me not to loan him money. Hakim is ungrateful and you simply cannot be nice to him and he feels that the world owes him something", Lucas said, shaking his head.

"Well Lucas, you tried to help and just charge it to the game of life. Don't loan him any more money and be more careful about the people that you do business with", Shelia said.

"Sometimes, family treats you worse than strangers."

"Sad, but true."

"Well, I've learned my lesson and that will never happen again", Lucas said, determined.

"Good", Shelia said.

A week later, Lucas and Shelia are sitting in the living room, conversating and waiting for Mayor Lane and Karen to arrive for dinner. The front doorbell rings and Lucas gets up from the living room sofa and looks through the window. He sees that it's Mayor Lane and Karen. and Lucas smiles and then opens the door and invites them in. He escorts them into the living room and when Shelia sees them, her face lights up. She rises up from the living room sofa and hugs them and Lucas encourages them to sit down. They thank him and sit down and Mayor Lane and Karen thank Lucas and Shelia for inviting them over.

"Mayor Lane, it's only fair that we invite you and Karen over. We had a great time at your residence and we wanted to return the favor", Lucas said.

"We appreciate this and your kind words", Mayor Lane said.

"Me too", Karen said.

"The food should be ready and I'm going to check on it", Shelia said.

"Okay honey", Lucas said.

Shelia goes into the kitchen and Lucas continues the conversation with Mayor Lane and Karen.

"Mayor Lane, what good legislation have you passed lately? Are you accomplishing everything that you want as Mayor?", Lucas asked.

"Well, we just passed legislation that would reduce property taxes in Butlerville. We also made stricter laws against loitering because businesses have been complaining. No mayor or elected official accomplishes everything that they want, but we give our best effort", Mayor Lane said.

"I can respect that and all we can do is give our best effort in life."

"Exactly."

"Karen, have you bought any new plants or antiques lately?", Lucas asked.

"No, and I've actually slowed down in buying them", Karen said.

"You have?"

"Yes, because my plants are beginning to clutter our home. Dugan has been getting on me about that and we've been talking about how we can expand our home."

"Really?"

"Lucas, we might expand our kitchen and front porch", Mayor Lane said.

"And I would like to paint our house a different color because I'm tired of it", Karen said.

"I can relate to that because our house could use some work, like some updated electrical work", Lucas said.

"In life there seems to be always a problem that needs to be solved."

"Yes, and as long as you live, there will always be problems."

"You're right."

"The food is ready and y' all can start filling your plates!", Shelia said.

Lucas escorts Mayor Lane and Karen into the kitchen. After everyone fixes their plates, they all sit down at the kitchen table. Before they begin eating, Lucas leads everyone in prayer and when he's finished, Karen speaks.

"Lucas and Shelia, the food smells and looks good", Karen said.

"It sure does", Mayor Lane agreed.

"Thank you and we hope that you and the Mayor like it", Shelia said.

"We worked together on it", Lucas said, proudly.

"We sure did", Shelia said, smiling at Lucas.

"The weather was nice today, wasn't it? Especially for this time of the year", Shelia said.

"It was so warm that I decided to wash our car today", Mayor Lane said.

"It was the perfect day to do something like that."

"It sure was."

"And the weather is supposed to be warm again tomorrow."

"Well then, I'm going to wash our car tomorrow", Lucas promised.

"And I can do some yard work", Karen said.

"I need to be doing that", Shelia said.

"This would be a good time to go fishing. Lucas, do you and Shelia fish?", Mayor Lane asked.

"Yeah I do, but I haven't fished in months", Lucas said.

"What about you Shelia?"

"Oh no! In all due respect, I don't have the patience for fishing. My father took me fishing when I was a kid and I found myself daydreaming."

"Karen, do you like fishing?", Lucas asked.

"I fish occasionally, but I don't love it as much as Dugan does."

"Where do you like to fish Lucas?" Do you have a favorite place?", Mayor Lane asked.

"I usually fish at Lake Shelbyville or Clinton Lake. For some reason, I have a lot of success in those places", Lucas said.

"Those are good places to fish. My favorite fishing spots are Lake Springfield and Lake Eureka."

"I don't like Lake Eureka because I don't have good fortune there. Maybe the lake doesn't like me", Lucas joked.

"Lucas, you probably just went there on the wrong day. If you fished there more, your luck would probably change", Mayor Lane suggested.

"Maybe", Lucas said, unconvinced.

"Lucas, I think that we should go fishing sometime. What do you think about that?", Mayor Lane asked.

"I think that's a great idea and when did you want to go?"

"I don't know because I have a lot of political obligations coming up. I'm pretty sure that you have important obligations too and I'll stay in touch with you Lucas. We can go when our schedules complement each other."

"Okay and I know that we're going to have a great time."

"I have no doubt about that. Mayor Lane, do you and Karen play spades? Would y' all like to play after dinner?", Lucas asked.

"I would love to play and what about you Karen?", Mayor Lane asked, looking at her.

"Sure, and we haven't played spades in a while. This should be fun", Karen said.

"Shelia, do you want to play spades too?", Lucas said, smiling at her.

"I would love to", Shelia said, returning the smile.

"What should we play up to?", Lucas asked.

"What about five hundred?", Karen asked.

"That's fine with me. How does everybody feel about that?"

After dinner is over, Lucas and Shelia partner against Mayor Lane and Karen. Lucas excuses himself and temporarily leaves and goes into the living room. He opens up a drawer and takes out a deck of cards and moments later, he re-enters the kitchen. Lucas sits down and asks everyone if they're okay with him dealing the cards. No one has a problem with it and Lucas gives everyone their cards counter clockwise. For a couple of hours, the teams exchange leads and finally, Mayor Lane defeat Lucas and Shelia. They conversate for thirty minutes after the game and then Mayor Lane and Karen decide to leave. They thank Lucas and Shelia for inviting them over and for a good time. Lucas and Shelia tell them that they're welcome and that they'll be in touch with them. Minutes later, Mayor Lane and Karen get into their car and a short time moments later, he drives off and heads toward Butlerville. A month later, Lucas is sitting at home alone in the living room while Shelia is still sleeping soundly on a Saturday morning. It's five-thirty a.m. and Lucas is waiting for Mayor Lane to arrive so that they can go fishing. While he's waiting, Lucas occupies his time by scanning various television channels. Five minutes later, Lucas hears a vehicle horn honking and he gets up and makes his way toward the front door. Lucas and pushes the curtain to the side and he sees a blue SUV outside and recognizes it as Mayor Lane's vehicle. He walks back to the living room to gather his fishing equipment and backpack. Moments later, Lucas leaves the house and closes the door behind him. He makes his way toward Mayor Lane's SUV and Mayor Lane greets Lucas pleasantly and he pops open his trunk. Mayor Lane encourages Lucas to put his equipment inside and he does so Lucas and he thanks Mayor Lane. A short time later, they enter the vehicle and before Mayor Lane drives off, Lucas asks him if they have all the necessary equipment.

"I think that we have everything that we need Lucas", Mayor Lane said.

"Do we have enough fish bait? Do we have corkers?", Lucas asked.

"I bought plenty of fish bait at Shelby's Fishing Store. I also bought a couple of new corkers to go along with my old ones. If we're not having good fishing luck with one corker, then we can try another one."

"That sounds good to me Mayor and I love the way that you're thinking."

"Lucas, I wanted us to fish at Lake Springfield. It's well known in Illinois for having a lot of catfish, walleye, bluegills, and various other fish. There's almost no good reason why we shouldn't have a successful fishing day", Mayor Lane reasoned.

"Everything that you've said makes sense", Lucas agreed.

"I love waking up early in the morning and admiring the beautiful sunrise. And I love hearing the birds chirping in their special language. To me, that's nature at its best."

"It is a beautiful morning. By the way Mayor, I have some snacks in my backpack for us. I have some potato chips, Cheetos, and some ham and cheese sandwiches."

"I appreciate that, Lucas. I brought us some hot dogs, Doritos, a two-liter of Sprite, and of course, some ice."

"Our stomachs will stay full and that will help our fishing concentration", Lucas said.

"Agreed. Lucas, are you ready to head up to Lake Springfield? Did you bring everything that you're going to need?", Mayor Lane asked.

Lucas pauses for a moment. He reflects on his fishing equipment and then indicates to Mayor Lane that he has everything. A short time later, Mayor Lane drives off and almost two hours later, he pulls into a shoreline and parks his vehicle. Mayor Lane and Lucas get out of the vehicle and take their fishing equipment out of the mayor's trunk and walk toward the edge of the lake. They put some of their items on the grass and before they begin fishing, Mayor Lane and Lucas admire the scenery that surrounds them.

"Lucas, one of the many reasons that I love fishing up here is because the scenery is so beautiful", Mayor Lane said.

"The water and trees look so healthy", Lucas said.

"Fishing is a great stress reliever for me."

"With your job Mayor Lane, you definitely need stress relievers."

"Not only that, but I know that I'm going to eat well", Mayor Lane said, rubbing his belly.

"Mayor Lane, are you ready to start fishing?", Lucas said, tying his hook on his fishing line.

"Almost."

Mayor Lane and Lucas finish setting up their fishing equipment. Minutes later, they both put their fishing poles into the lake and patiently wait for fish to nibble on their hooks. Almost immediately, a fish tugs on Mayor Lane's hook and he attempts to reel it in. As he's trying to reel the fish in, it escapes his hook and swims away. Mayor Lane is disgusted.

"Damn Lucas! I tried to reel in that fish too soon and I lost it!"

"Calm down Mayor because the day is young. I'm sure that you'll more than make up for it."

"You're right and that's a great way of looking at it."

"It happens to the best of us."

"Some of the best memories of my childhood are of me and my father fishing. He used to participate in fishing tournaments throughout Illinois and he was pretty good", Mayor Lane bragged.

"I can imagine that you're a pretty good fisherman too Mayor", Lucas said.

"Well, I'm okay. My father taught me so much, not only about fishing, but about life. I think about him every day. Lucas, when was the last time that you talked to your parents?"

"I talked to them a couple of days ago and they're doing fine."

"Good. Enjoy and cherish your parents and always honor them. None of us knows when God is going to call us home."

"I will Mayor and thank you for sharing that with me."

"You're welcome, Lucas. Your corker just went under the water and you have a fish that's ready to be caught!"

"I'm going to catch this sucker", Lucas said, determined.

Lucas turns his attention toward the lake and a fish is jerking his pole. He calmly reels it toward him and then Lucas sees that he has caught the fish and Lucas smiles proudly. He takes the fish off the hook and a short time later; Lucas is holding the fish with both hands and it's a catfish. He shows it to Mayor Lane and he smiles and nods his head approvingly. Lucas puts the catfish into a cooler of ice and then Mayor Lane speaks to Lucas.

"Lucas, you caught one whopper of a catfish!"

"I can't wait to eat that bad boy!"

"This could be a good sign", Mayor Lane said, hopefully.

"I hope so", Lucas said.

"This is a great example of why I love fishing up here. Most of the time, the fish really bite", Mayor Lane said.

"Maybe I should fish up here more often", Lucas said.

"Lucas, I feel a fish tugging my hook!"

"Don't let it get away Mayor!"

Mayor Lane concentrates on reeling in the fish. Moments later, he removes the fish from his hook and he sees thar it's his favorite fish, a walleye. that it's his favorite fish, walleye. His face is beaming with pride and he shows it to Lucas. He salutes the mayor with a huge smile and two thumbs up. A short time later, Mayor Lane places his walleye into the iced cooler and then he and Lucas continue fishing. They fish until the early afternoon before finally calling it quits. They're pleased at the number of fish that they have caught and they travel back to Center City. Almost two hours later, they arrive there and Mayor Lane is parking his vehicle in front of Lucas' home. After he's parked, the mayor turns off his engine and they get out of the vehicle and walk toward the trunk. Mayor Lane opens the trunk and Lucas takes out his fishing equipment and backpack. Before entering his home, Lucas thanks the mayor for an enjoyable time.

"Lucas, you're welcome and I enjoyed fishing as much as you did. We should do this more often", Mayor Lane suggested.

"I agree and Lake Springfield is a great place to fish. I haven't done that well in a long time", Lucas said.

"We can definitely go back up there", Mayor Lane said.

"I'm looking forward to it", Lucas said.

"Lucas, I'm going to head back to Butlerville. Tell your family that I said hello."

"I sure will Mayor and tell your family the same."

"Good-bye Lucas."

"Good-bye Mayor."

Mayor Lane gets back into his vehicle and a short time later, drives off. Moments later, Lucas walks into the house and is greeted warmly by Shelia.

"Honey, how was your fishing day?", Shelia asked.

"It was great and I enjoyed myself!", Lucas said excitedly.

"That's great!"

"We caught a variety of different fish. I have some catfish, walleye, and bluegill. We're going to have plenty of fish for a while."

"You know how much our family loves fish."

"I know and it's going to be great eating."

"Lucas, how is Mayor Lane doing?", Shelia asked.

"He's doing fine and told me to tell our family hello", Lucas said.

"That's good and I appreciate that."

"Did anything unusual happen in the neighborhood while I was gone?"

"No, it has been quiet and peaceful."

"Good. Shelia, I'm going to freshen up and change my clothes. After that, I'm going to gut, wrap, and ice the fish and then freeze them.

"Lucas, after you finish freshening up, maybe you should get something to eat. You've had a long day", Shelia suggested.

"I will Shelia. I still have a couple of bologna sandwiches and Pepsi's left from the fishing trip. I'll have that", Lucas said.

"No need to do all that work on an empty stomach", Shelia reasoned.

"You're right Shelia."

Nothing special happens the rest of the day. Three years later, it's a beautiful, sunny October day and the temperature is in the fifties. Lucas' work day has ended and rather than go directly home, he decides to visit Mayor Lane's office. Before he does, Lucas decides to stop off at Kroger's to pick up some items. Lucas purchases some ground beef and Manwich for his family and some apples and oranges for the mayor. He leaves the store and ten minutes later, Lucas arrives at Mayor Lane's office and he's greeted warmly by the mayor's secretary Mary Stanford. Lucas asks her if the mayor is there and if he's busy and she tells him to wait while she contacts him. Lucas nods his head and thanks her and a short time later, Mary gives Lucas's permission to enter Mayor Lane's office. Lucas thanks her and makes his way toward the mayor's office. When Lucas walks in, the mayor's face breaks out into a huge smile and they greet each other and exchange steel grip handshakes. Mayor Lane points to a chair in front of his desk and urges Lucas to sit down. Before Lucas sits down, he gives the mayor the apples and oranges. Mayor Lane is pleasantly surprised at the kind gesture and thanks him. Lucas asks the mayor how he's been.

"Well, it's been more difficult for me to get out of bed in the morning. Sometimes, I have to ask Karen to help me and I have trouble keeping my balance while I'm walking", Mayor Lane said.

"Have you been doing your stretching exercises daily? Have you been sticking to your diet?", Lucas asked, concerned.

"I have been doing my stretching exercises, but I've been slacking on my diet."

"Mayor Lane, you have to eat healthier. Hopefully, these apples and oranges will help you refocus on your diet."

"I appreciate you going out of your way for me Lucas. I appreciate your concern for me."

"It was no problem Mayor Lane. How is your family?", Lucas asked.

"Well, considering my condition, they're doing alright. I feel like I'm a burden to my family and I hate feeling like this", Mayor Lane said, frustrated.

"Mayor Lane, you have a wonderful family that loves you very much. They honor you and they're going to do everything they can to help you." My family and the residents of Butlerville love you and you're not alone."

"I know, but lately, I've been more depressed."

"We're here for you Mayor Lane and our support isn't going anywhere", Lucas promised.

"I feel better just by hearing you say that", Mayor Lane said, letting out a long sigh.

"Good."

"Lucas, how is your family? How is everything going at B. Mitchell?"

"My family is alright and Shelia received a raise at her job. Chester and Melvin are both honor roll students and things are going well for me at B. Mitchell."

"That's great. I remember watching Bradley playing against Indiana State last year. Chester had a great game and I remember him scoring thirty points. Lucas, is Melvin on the debate team at Southern Illinois?", Mayor Lane asked.

"No, Melvin isn't, but he loves his university. He majored in Education and Shelia and I have no doubt that he's going to be a great teacher. Speaking of basketball, I can only imagine how proud you and Karen must be of Mark and Kevin", Lucas said.

"You're right Lucas. I feel great that Mark chose my alma mater, the University of Illinois at Champaign. Karen and I didn't put any pressure on him to attend my alma mater. We made it very clear to him that we would support whatever decision he made. Mark is majoring in Finance and Kevin is attending the University of Michigan at Ann Arbor and he's majoring in Political Science. We have two sons attending big ten universities and what are the odds of that?"

"Wow! I never thought about something like that. They're both attending great universities."

"So are Chester and Melvin. Lucas, having you show up like this has really brightened my day", Mayor Lane said, smiling.

"I'm happy that you feel that way and thank you for the kind words", Lucas said, graciously.

"Is there anything that I can help you with Lucas?"

"I'm fine Mayor Lane and I appreciate you asking."

"No problem Lucas."

"Well, Mayor Lane, I'm going to head home now. I just wanted to check on you", Lucas said.

"I appreciate your friendship Lucas and drive home safely", Mayor Lane said.

"I will."

They both rise up from their chairs and shake hands and then Lucas walks out and heads home. A month later, Lucas and Shelia are at home and are having a conversation about Chester and Melvin.

"I just got off the phone talking to Chester and Melvin and they're both low on money. I told them that I was going to wire them some money when I finished talking to them. I'm going to Western Union right now and do you want to come along Shelia?", Lucas asked.

"Sure, and I could use some fresh air", Shelia said.

"Okay."

Lucas and Shelia get up and leave and when they arrive at Western Union, Lucas walks in while Shelia remains in the car. Lucas walks over to a counter and sees various forms on it and scans them for the Send Money forms. When he sees them, Lucas takes a couple of them out of a pile and then picks up a nearby ink pen and begins filling out the forms. When he's finished, Lucas takes the completed forms to a cashier and he gives her six hundred dollars, with Chester and Melvin receiving three hundred dollars each. When the transaction is completed, Lucas walks out and rejoins Shelia in the car. Before he drives off, Shelia asks Lucas to stop off at Walgreen's before they head home. He obliges and a short time later, Lucas pulls into the Walgreen's parking lot and Shelia gets out of the car and walks in. Lucas waits for her in the car and Shelia walks to the Beauty Care aisle. She picks up some Sta Soft Fro hair spray, eye liner, a comb, and some lipstick. Shelia walks up to a cashier and gives her a Walgreen's Balance Rewards Card. The cashier rings up her items and then scans her card and registers her discount. Moments later, Shelia walks out and heads toward the car. and before heading home, Lucas asks her if she needs to go anywhere else. Shelia thanks him for asking and then tells him no and Lucas starts up the car and heads home. A couple of hours later, the phone rings and Shelia answers it and it's Chester.

"Hello Chester and how are you son?", Shelia asked.

"I'm fine Mom and how are you and Dad? What's going on in Center City?", Chester asked.

"We're okay and still working every day. They're going to be opening up a Walmart in Center City, not far from us."

"When is it supposed to open?"

"Sometime next month. I almost forgot to tell you that your old high school defeated Jackson Lutheran last night, seventy-four to fifty-seven."

"That's great news."

"When was the last time that you talked with Melvin?", Shelia asked.

"I talked to him a couple of days ago and he was doing fine. He had just come from the library after studying for his History exam", Chester said.

"That's good."

"Mom, I thank you and Dad for sending that money and I really appreciate it."

"No problem Chester and we had a feeling that your money was leaking."

"That money was right on time and I was down to my last ten dollars. Mom, is Dad around?", Chester asked.

"Yes, he is and do you want to speak with him?", Shelia asked.

"Yeah I would."

"Hold on Chester."

"Okay."

"Lucas! Chester is on the phone and he wants to talk to you!", Shelia said.

"I'll be right there!", Lucas said.

Moments later, Lucas walks out of their bedroom and joins Shelia in the living room. Lucas is smiling from ear-to-ear as he accepts the phone from Shelia. He thanks her and then speaks to Chester.

"Hello Chester! I'm so happy that you called son and are you okay?", Lucas asked.

"I'm alright and are you okay Dad?", Chester asked.

"Never been better."

"Dad, I thank you and Mom for sending that money."

"You're welcome and if you need more, don't hesitate to call us."

"I'll keep that in mind Dad", Chester promised.

"How's college life going?"

"It's going smoothly and we've won three games in a row. Yesterday, we defeated the University of Cincinnati, eighty-three to seventy-nine."

"That's good Chester. Have you been keeping up your grades?"

"Yeah and I'm on the honor roll. A couple of days ago, I received an A on my Science exam."

"We're proud of you son and keep up the great work. Chester, we've made some changes at home", Lucas said.

"Like what?", Chester asked.

"We bought a new refrigerator and a living room set. Nothing lasts forever and we were tired of having problems with the refrigerator. And the new furniture brings a fresh look to our living room."

"I love hearing that."

"Chester, I---"

Lucas hears someone trying to call him on the other end of the line. He frowns and tells Chester to hold on while he checks to see whom it is and its Melvin. Lucas smiles and then tells Chester that its Melvin and that he'll finish talking to him later. Chester hangs up and Lucas clicks over and begins talking to Melvin.

"Hello Melvin and it's great to hear your voice. How's son number two?", Lucas asked.

"I'm fine Dad number one and how's everything on the home front?", Melvin asked.

"Everything is good."

"How's Mom?"

"She's okay."

"I thank you and Mom for sending that money and I feel much better", Melvin said.

"Some extra funds always help. You might want to attend some event or maybe take out a young lady", Lucas said.

"You're right."

"I was talking to Chester when you called. We're happy that both of you are doing okay."

"And we're happy that you and Mom are doing fine."

Shelia gets Lucas' attention and she pretends to hold a phone against her ear. Shelia indicates to Lucas that she wants to talk to Melvin when he's finished. Lucas nods his head approvingly and he talks to Melvin for another ten minutes before he gives the phone to Shelia.

"Melvin, I'm glad that you called. Do you need anything? Are you okay?", Shelia asked.

"I'm alright and still on the Honor Roll. Things are going well, knock on wood", Melvin said.

"That's great Melvin. Be careful and pay attention to your surroundings. There are some crazy people in this world."

"I will Mom."

"Are you and your roommate getting along?"

"Me and Ricky are getting along and we haven't been having problems."

"I've been watching the news lately. It seems like there's been more violence on college campuses", Shelia said, concerned.

"I appreciate your concern Mom and I'm alright", Melvin assured her.

"Okay."

"Mom, I'm going to get off now because I need to begin studying for my Calculus exam. I'll be in touch with you and Dad."

"Alright and I enjoyed talking to Melvin and we love you."

"Love y' all too Mom and good-bye", Melvin said.

"Good-bye Melvin."

Nothing special happens the rest of the day. Two months later, Lucas and Shelia are visiting the mayor's residence. They're sitting in the living room and talking with Karen while Mayor Lane is nearby sitting in a wheelchair. He is quiet and has breathing tubes inserted up his nose, but is aware of his surroundings. Karen is having trouble dealing with the reality of Mayor Lane's condition and indicates this to Lucas and Shelia.

"I hate to see Dugan like this and he's only a shadow of himself. I'm used to seeing my husband active and being a fireball of energy. I don't know how to handle this", Karen admitted.

"When I think of Mayor Lane, I think of a good man and a loyal friend. I think of his positive, can-do attitude and our lives have definitely been richer because of him", Lucas said.

"Mayor Lane is a special man and you don't find people like him every day", Shelia said.

"Our sons are taking Dugan's condition so hard and I feel so helpless! There's nothing that I can do about it!", Karen said, with tears rolling down her cheeks.

"We're here for you and your family", Shelia said.

"We're going to make Dugan's last days as comfortable as possible. He's been having muscle cramps and now he's starting to have breathing problems", Karen said.

"Call us if we can be of any help", Lucas said.

"Thank you and I don't know what I would do without y' all. We love y' all and your friendship means so much to us", Karen said, thankfully.

"Same here Karen and it's time for a group hug", Shelia said.

They all rise up and exchange kisses, hugs, and tears. When they're finished, they continue talking for another half an hour before Lucas and Shelia head home. The rest of the day is uneventful and three weeks later, on a Monday night, Lucas is at home watching Blackish while Shelia is at work. He's chowing down on a bag of Cheetos Cheese Puffs and during a commercial break, the phone rings. Lucas gets up from the living room sofa to see whom it is. When he sees the number on the Caller ID, its Mayor Lane's number appearing. An uncomfortable feeling comes over Lucas lets out a sigh of dread and then answers it. Mayor Lane's wife Karen is on the other end of the line.

"Hello", Lucas said.

"Hello Lucas, this is Karen", she said.

"Karen, how's everything?"

"Not that good. Dugan passed away a couple of hours ago and God took him home."

"I'm so sorry to hear that. He's not suffering anymore and he's at peace."

"I'm going to miss him so much. I loved Dugan with every bit of my heart and soul. He was a great husband, father, and mayor", Karen said.

"He was definitely all those things. We were blessed for him to have been a part of our lives", Lucas said.

"Our sons are now without their father and I feel so bad for them. I---

At that point, Karen loses her composure and can no longer control her emotions. She begins crying uncontrollably and Lucas does his best to console her. He encourages Karen to reflect on the good memories that she had with Mayor Lane and after crying for minutes, Karen regains her composure. She gathers her thoughts and thanks Lucas for being patient.

"No problem Karen and you needed to let those emotions out", Lucas said.

"Lucas, I'll be in contact with you and Shelia about Dugan's funeral arrangements", Karen promised.

"Okay Karen and we'll definitely be there. Do y' all need anything?"

"No Lucas. You've done a lot just by talking to me. Thank you."

"Stay in touch with us."

"I will Lucas and good night", Karen said.

"Good night", Lucas said.

Lucas hangs up and later that night, Lucas and Shelia are in bed discussing Mayor Lane's death.

"Lucas, I feel so bad for Mayor Lane's family. I'm going to call Karen tomorrow and offer my condolences", Shelia said.

"I told her to contact us if they needed anything. She's going to let us know when and where Mayor Lane's funeral will be. I'll be praying for them", Lucas said.

"Me too."

A week later, Lucas is at home and the phone rings and it's Karen. Lucas answers it and after they exchange hellos, she gives Lucas information about Mayor Lane's funeral.

"Lucas, Dugan's funeral will take place at one o' clock at Zion Baptist Church this coming Saturday in Butlerville. It's about four blocks west of Butlerville High School", Karen said.

"We'll be there", Lucas promised.

"Thank you, Lucas. You and Shelia might want to leave the house maybe an hour before the service. We're expecting a huge sendoff for Dugan and there are going to be many dignitaries, family, and friends at his funeral."

"That's exactly what Mayor Lane deserves and we'll do that."

"We're looking forward to seeing y' all there. Well Lucas, I'm going to get off the phone now and I just wanted to give y' all an update of the funeral arrangements."

"Okay Karen and we appreciate that. See y' all then and good-bye."

"Good-bye Lucas."

A week later, Lucas and Shelia are at the church and they're scanning the crowd while walking toward the church entrance. The funeral has the appearance of a Who's Who of Illinois. They see Governor Pete Thompson, United States Senator Omar "Teddy Bear" Johnson, Poet Laureate Ann Howard, Television Talk Show Host Princess Rogers, and numerous other dignitaries. Lucas and Shelia make their way into the church and are escorted to a row in the back of the church. They conversate with each other and some mourners while they stand and wait for the funeral proceedings to start. While everyone is waiting, two United States Military Soldiers walk toward the mayor's open casket. When they arrive at it, the soldiers place a United States Flag and an Illinois State Flag on opposite ends of Mayor Lane's casket. The soldiers turn and face each other briefly in silence and then salute each other before walking away. Mayor Lane's family, relatives, and other dignitaries walk onto a stage behind Pastor Bob Zimmer's podium and sit down in designated chairs. A short time later, everyone sits down and the funeral begins and Pastor Zimmer opens his Bible and turns to John, Chapter fourteen. When he's finished reading and translating scriptures, various family members, relatives, friends, and dignitaries express their love, admiration, and respect for the life that Mayor

Lane lived. After they're finished speaking, Pastor Zimmer asks the choir to sing various songs and they comply. The last song they perform is "Amazing Grace" and mourners gradually make their way toward Mayor Lane's open casket. When Karen arrives at the casket, she bursts out crying uncontrollably and she tries to climb into the casket. But, her sons Mark, Kevin, and other mourners pull her back. Mark and Kevin are also sobbing and then Karen yells out, "Dugan! Dugan! I want to join you with the Lord! Let me join you!" Once again, Karen tries to climb into the casket and she's pulled back again. Moments later, Karen faints and her sons catch her before she hits the ground and they and other mourners try to revive and console her. The choir continues to sing and they're finally able to revive Karen and half a dozen United States Military Soldiers approach the mayor's casket. Two of them gently close Mayor Lane's casket and the soldiers escort his body outside where he is placed in a funeral home car. Mayor Lane and Karen's family, relatives, and close dignitaries get into the car and a short time later, the funeral car pulls off and heads toward Mayor Lane's final resting place. Three months later, on a beautiful Spring Day, Lucas and Shelia are outside at home. They're in the backyard and preparing for their neighborhood cookout and discussing how much they're looking forward to it.

"Shelia, I believe that this cookout is going to be great! It's going to feel great to have family and good friends over", Lucas said, while pouring some charcoal into his grill chimney starter.

"This is a great day for it because the weather is so nice", Shelia said, looking toward the sky.

"It is and I hope that everyone enjoys themselves."

"I believe that they will. What great foods are you going to grill today, Lucas?"

"I'm going to grill some hot dogs, hamburgers, and some baby back ribs."

"Yummy!"

"I almost forgot that I have to go to the store get some beverages", Lucas said, snapping a finger.

"Lucas, you don't have to worry about. I went to the store while you were sleeping and I bought a variety of drinks. We have Kool-Aid, Sodas, and Beer", Shelia said.

"Thank you, Shelia. That's one less thing that we have to worry about. Do you think that we have enough plates, cups, and napkins?"

"We should and if we don't, there's a grocery store right around the corner."

"Can you think of anything else that we might need?"

"No, I think that we have everything that we need. What food are you going to start grilling first?", Shelia asked.

"I think that I'm going to start off with the hot dogs. Shelia, I'm loving this new grill!", Lucas said, lighting up the charcoals.

"I'm happy to see you grilling with it", Shelia said.

"Do you know where Chester and Melvin are?"

"They're with friends and they'll be here later."

"Good."

Two hours later, Lucas and Shelia have finished preparing their cookout. They're sitting together on their back porch and enjoying each other's company. They're waiting for people to begin arriving and Lucas turns to Shelia and thanks her for helping him organize the cookout.

"Shelia, it would've been a lot more difficult to prepare this cookout without your help. I love and appreciate you Shelia", Lucas said, kissing her on the lips.

"Aw Lucas, that's so sweet of you and I feel the same way about you. Like I've always said, we're a team and we should help each other win", Shelia said, kissing Lucas back.

"We do make a great team and so do Chester and Melvin."

"It's a blessing to have them as our sons and they've made us so proud."

"They sure have."

They continue conversating for another ten minutes and then they see a brown car parking near their yard. Lucas recognizes the driver of the car as his cousin Hakim. His cheery facial expression changes into displeasure and Lucas lets out a long sigh. A short time later, Hakim greets Lucas and Shelia and Lucas struggles to hide his displeasure of seeing Hakim. After greeting them, Hakim compliments them on their cookout setup.

"Y' all should pat yourselves on the back. The cookout arrangement looks great and the food smells terrific", Hakim said.

"Thank you, Hakim,", Shelia said.

"You're welcome. I know that the food is going to taste great and I might gain some weight before everyone's eyes", Hakim joked.

"We wouldn't mind being responsible for that", Shelia said, laughing.

"I have something for you Lucas", Hakim said.

"You do?", Lucas asked, surprised.

"Yeah I do", Hakim said, reaching into one of his pants pockets.

Hakim pulls out two hundred and fifty dollars and points the money toward Lucas. Hakim urges him to accept it and Lucas is shocked. He opens his mouth wider than normal. and moments later, he comes out of his shocked state of mind. Lucas accepts the money from Hakim and thanks him and then Hakim speaks to Lucas.

"Lucas, I thought long and hard about what you said on the phone. I owe you a huge apology and I'm sorry. We're family and I should've done the right thing by you and paid you back sooner. I promise that I'll treat you better from now on and I hope that you accept my apology", Hakim said, remorsefully.

"Hakim, this is a pleasant surprise. I accept your apology and I have a greater respect for you as a man. It takes a big man to admit when he's wrong", Lucas said.

"Thank you, Lucas."

"I'm puzzled as to why you gave me extra money."

"I did that because I was an asshole and I wanted to make things right with you."

"That's honorable Hakim. I think that it's time for a family hug."

"I agree."

Lucas and Hakim hug and pat each other on the back and then Shelia encourages Hakim to fix himself a plate. He is reluctant, but Shelia insists.

"Hakim, you're the first one to arrive and you might as well fix yourself a plate. You have the first chance at all this food and I know that you didn't come over here not to eat. We have plenty", Shelia said.

"Well, since you put it that way, I'll fix myself a plate", Hakim said.

"Knock yourself out Hakim", Lucas said.

"Okay", Hakim said, laughing.

Hakim walks over to the table of food and beverages and fixes himself a plate. And then he picks up a Budweiser and walks over to a nearby folding chair and sits down. Hakim places his beer down on the ground and then he begins eating. Minutes later, Lucas and Shelia fix their plates and then sit next to Hakim and they all conversate about various topics. Ten minutes later, they see Chester and Melvin arriving, along with two attractive young ladies. They also see Lucas' younger brother, Alvin Lightfoot and his wife Deborah Lightfoot. A short time later, everyone greets each other and share hugs and then Chester and Melvin introduce the young ladies to everyone.

"Everybody, this is my girlfriend, Kenya. Kenya, and this is my father, mother, and cousin Hakim", Chester said, pointing them out.

"Nice to meet y' all", Kenya said, pleasantly.

"Same here", Lucas said, smiling.

"And this is my girlfriend Veronica everyone", Melvin said, proudly.

"Hello everyone", Veronica said, shyly.

"Nice to meet you young ladies. We have plenty of food and drinks and help yourselves", Shelia said.

"I look forward to filling my belly", Alvin said, massaging his stomach.

"I can imagine", Lucas said, laughing.

"Deborah, I see that you have a bun in the oven", Shelia said, pointing toward her belly.

"Yes, and I am four months pregnant", Deborah said, laughing and looking down at her belly.

"That's a blessing. How is your pregnancy coming along?"

"The doctor told us that everything appears to be on schedule, knock on wood."

"That's good."

"Alvin has been so supportive and he stays on me to do what's necessary, even when I don't want too", Deborah said.

"I just want to make sure that Deborah's pregnancy goes as smoothly as possible", Alvin said.

"And you're doing a great job Alvin", Deborah said, winking at him.

"Thank you, Deborah,", Alvin said, winking back at her.

"You're welcome."

"That's being a damn good husband and I salute you Alvin", Lucas said, glowing with pride.

"I appreciate that Lucas", Alvin said.

"I can feel my appetite kicking in. Does everybody else feel like this?", Lucas asked, looking around.

Everyone indicates to Lucas and Shelia that they're ready to eat. They load up their plates and help themselves to various beverages. As they're eating and conversating, various relatives, friends, and neighbors begin arriving. Lucas and Shelia play a variety of old school and new school music and some people are dancing and clowning to the music. Others are joking and laughing with each other and Lucas, Shelia, Alvin, and Deborah are slow dancing and reflecting back on great memories. Children are running around without a care in the world and some of the boys are playing a game of cans. Others are playing basketball or throwing around a football. Some of the girls are playing double-dutch or sharing fashion advice. Three hours later, everyone begins to gradually leave and thank Lucas and Shelia for a great time. They thank everyone for coming over and after everyone has left, Lucas and Shelia begin gathering up the rest of the foods and beverages. They take them into the house and as they're doing this, Lucas sees his father and mother pull up in their vehicle. He is delighted and he puts down a pan of hot dogs on a table and walks toward their vehicle to greet them. They exchange hugs and as Lucas escorts them toward their house, his mother apologizes to Lucas for not showing up sooner.

"Mom, God bless your heart. I know that you haven't been feeling well and you could've stayed home", Lucas said.

"I felt guilty and I wanted to come over and enjoy my family. I just didn't have the energy to get over here earlier", Mom said.

"We would've understood", Lucas assured her.

"Lucas, you know how determined and stubborn your mother can be. When she makes up her mind to do something, she does everything in her power to accomplish it", Dad said.

"Dad, you tried to talk Mom into staying home, didn't you?", Lucas asked.

"I did and I failed big time", Dad joked.

"I know and there was no talking her out of it."

"Exactly."

"I hate that we missed everybody and did they enjoy themselves?", Mom asked.

"They sure did and it was a pleasure for us to host it", Lucas said, proudly.

"That's good."

"We were just taking everything into the house and we have plenty of food left. Mom and Dad, I want y' all to join us and chow down on this great food. Don't be shy and Shelia will be thrilled to see y' all. I--

"Mama and Daddy Lightfoot, it's great to see y' all", Shelia said, walking out of the house.

Shelia walks over to them and they all embrace and exchange greetings. Shelia asks them how they're feeling.

"Shelia, I feel much better than I did earlier today. I drank a Sprite earlier and it helped calm my stomach", Mama Lightfoot said.

"I'm glad that you're feeling better", Shelia said.

"Me too."

"Daddy Lightfoot, how are you?"

"I'm doing great", Daddy Lightfoot said.

"Good."

"Shelia, I told Mom and Dad to help themselves to our food", Lucas said.

"By all means, fill up your bellies", Shelia encouraged them.

"Thank y' all and I'll accept your offer", Mama Lightfoot said.

"I'll second that", Daddy Lightfoot said.

"Do y' all want to eat inside or outside?", Lucas asked.

"It doesn't matter to me Lucas. What do you think Denise?"

"I feel the same way Aaron."

"Well, since we've started taking the food inside, we might as well eat in the house", Lucas reasoned.

"I don't have a problem with that."

"Neither do I", Aaron said.

"Okay, let's go inside and start chowing down!", Lucas said.

They all walk into the house and head toward the kitchen and load up their plates. When they're finished, everyone sits down at the kitchen table and Lucas leads them in prayer. When he's finished, everyone begins eating and a short time later, Lucas asks his mother a question.

"Mom, when was the last time that you had a physical?", Lucas asked.

"Almost six months ago. Why do you ask?", Mom asked defensively.

"I'm just concerned Mom."

"I appreciate your concern son, but your Mother is fine. Why don't we talk about something else, like this wonderful food?"

"Okay, I'll get off the subject."

"Dad, when was the last time that you talked to our old neighbor Harry Stevens?", Lucas asked.

"I talked to him a couple of days ago and he's doing okay. Do you remember Meesha Holder?", Dad asked.

"I sure do and she was always a nice lady."

"Well, Harry and Meesha recently became engaged."

"They've been dating? Really? That's great news and I'm happy for them."

"Yep. They've been together for almost two years and they decided to tie the knot", Dad said.

"It's always good when great things happen for good people", Lucas said.

"It sure is."

"These baby back ribs are really good", Mom said, smacking her lips.

"Thank you, Mom,", Lucas said, beaming.

"You're welcome son."

"Shelia, how is your family?", Dad asked.

"Thank you for asking and everyone is fine. My youngest sister Belinda recently earned her CDL to become a Semi-Truck Driver and she's excited about the opportunity", Shelia said, proudly.

"That's great and tell her that we said congratulations."

"I'll be sure to tell her that."

"That's a great achievement and I've never known a woman Semi-Truck driver", Mom said.

"I know what you mean. She's the first one in our family to do this and we're so proud of her", Shelia said.

"Y' all should be."

"Belinda has always enjoyed nature and adventure and this job fits the bill for her."

"Life is so much better when you're able to do things that you enjoy."

"Yes indeed."

"These hot dogs and potato salad are delicious", Dad said.

"Dad, Shelia deserves the credit for the hot dogs. Our good neighbor Gloria brought over the potato salad", Lucas said.

"They did a great job."

"Lucas and I worked together as a team."

"Well Shelia y' all won the food championship of the world", Dad quipped.

"i second that", Mom said.

"Your words have made my day", Shelia said, glowing.

"Shelia, have you checked out any new television shows lately?", Mom asked.

"No, but I'm still addicted to Empire and Star. There's always so much drama and suspense in their episodes!", Shelia said, enthusiastically.

"I love those shows too and I also love Saints and Sinners. Those characters really live up to the title of the show."

"I love seeing black shows like these and I hope to see more like them."

"Me too."

Everyone becomes temporarily silent and enjoy the food and then Lucas speaks to his father.

"Dad, I'm happy that your car is up and running again. What was wrong with it?", Lucas asked.

"I took my car up to Dave's Auto Shop. Dave told me that I needed a tune-up, transmission work, and some brakes. The breaks were starting to show some serious wear and tear", Dad said.

"Thank God that you caught the problem with your brakes because that's no joke."

"I know and I told Dave to replace them and my brakes work so much better."

"I know that you're happy to be driving again."

"I sure am. I'm thankful that I have a warranty and it's good for another two years."

"That's good", Lucas said.

"I try to stay on top of my business", Dad said.

"I try and do the same, just like you", Lucas said, pointing toward him.

"Thank you for the compliment Lucas and it warms my heart", Dad said.

Everyone continues eating and conversating for another hour and then Lucas' parents decide to leave. On their way out, everyone embraces each other and Lucas and Shelia tell them to buckle up and drive home safely. They appreciate their concerned words and his parents assure them that they will follow their suggestions. Moments later, they leave and make their way toward their car and a short time later, Lucas' father drives off.

CHAPTER FIVE

The Final Destination

It's a July afternoon and Lucas and Shelia are at home. They're sitting on the living room sofa and talking to each other and during their conversation, Lucas makes a big announcement.

"Shelia, I've thought about everything that you've said. I'm going to run for Mayor of Butlerville", Lucas said.

"I had a feeling that you would and I'm happy that you decided to do it", Shelia said, proudly.

"I don't know the first thing about running for public office. But before he died, Mayor Lane told me that his campaign manager Clarence Backman was outstanding. I'm going to reach out to him."

"You should do that Lucas and I believe that God is going to surround you with the right people."

"Do you know what time it is Shelia?", Lucas asked.

"It's four o' clock", Shelia said, looking at her watch.

"Great! Clarence is still in his office and I'm going to call him right now!"

"Go for it Lucas!"

Lucas picks up the phone and dials Clarence's number and it rings three times before he answers it.

"Hello", Clarence said.

"Hello Clarence, this is Lucas Lightfoot. How are you?", Lucas asked.

"I'm fine and this is a pleasant surprise. Is everything good with you?", Clarence asked.

"Everything is alright."

"Good. Is there something that I can do for you Lucas?"

"Yes, there is. I've decided to run for Mayor of Butlerville and I could use your help."

"That's great Lucas and Mayor Lane always spoke highly of you. Have you talked this over with Shelia?"

"Not exactly. I just literally told her that I was going to run for Mayor. I don't know where to start."

"I am willing to help you Lucas. I have to finish up some paperwork here and I should be done by about five o' clock. Would it be okay if I came by and talked to you and Shelia?", Clarence asked.

"Sure. Just come on through", Lucas said.

"Good and I'll probably arrive there at around five-thirty, or maybe a quarter to six."

"Sounds good to me Clarence and we'll see you then. Good-bye."

"Good-bye Lucas."

At a quarter to six, Clarence arrives and he's greeted warmly by Lucas and Shelia. Before they all sit down, Shelia asks Clarence if he wants something to drink. He thanks Shelia for her offer and then politely declines. They all sit down on the living room sofa and then Clarence begins talking to Lucas.

"Lucas, I know that it's tough running for public office, especially when it's your first time. I'm going to help you and I want to start by asking you one basic question", Clarence said.

"What is it?", Lucas asked.

"Why do you want to be the Mayor of Butlerville?"

"I want to unite the citizens of Butlerville and bring the town into the twenty-first century. I want to bring in more family supporting jobs, fix the terrible potholes on our streets, and increase funding for schools so that students can have more access to modern technology. If I am elected Mayor, I am going to do everything that I can to replace that street name, Robert E. Lee Boulevard. That's a terrible thing for people of goodwill to see when they enter Butlerville. I want good people of all races and backgrounds to feel welcome. To paraphrase that great quote by Doctor Martin Luther King Junior, we should live in a nation in which we're not judged by the color of our skin, but by the content of our character. This is twenty-eighteen, not nineteen sixty-eight."

"That's admirable Lucas. Mayor Lane tried for many years to have the name of that boulevard removed, but was not successful. He could never get enough votes from the town council members. What makes you believe that you can Lucas?"

"Well, I don't know Clarence, but I'm going to give my best effort to have it removed. Butlerville city council members are up for re-election and maybe they will elect more progressive elected officials", Lucas said.

"I like your positive attitude Lucas and maybe things will change", Clarence said.

"Clarence, what can I do to help Lucas succeed?", Shelia asked.

"I appreciate that question Shelia. That makes me feel even better about Lucas' chances of becoming Mayor."

"Thank you."

"To answer your question, you can help Lucas pass out flyers. You could also do some door-to-door campaigning with him and me and my and staff will obviously help", Clarence assured her.

"I'll support Lucas in any way that I can", Shelia promised.

"Do either of you have any experience creating websites?"

"Well, I don't specifically, but I did earn a certificate for basic computer operations at the Center City Library", Shelia said.

"As a supervisor at B. Mitchell, I have to use a computer daily in order to keep track of production", Lucas said.

"Well, I'm going to help both of you develop a first-class website. It will help Lucas explain his future vision for Butlerville and help the voters know more about him. It's very important to build trust with potential voters."

"I'm happy that I called you Clarence and I feel much better about running for Mayor."

"I'm glad that I could be of assistance", Clarence said.

"Me too", Shelia said.

"Lucas, my staff and I are going to coach you on how to effectively communicate with the news media. This is very important because they are going to ask you tough questions and you have to be able to handle the pressure. In other words, I want you to be prepared for anything that you might face during your campaign. Nate Greenburg is an experienced politician and he's probably going to pull some tricks on you."

"This might be a problem because of my work schedule."

"I know and we can talk more about this in detail. I can talk to your boss and we can work something out. Do y' all have any other questions?", Clarence asked.

"Not that I can think of right now. Shelia, do you have any questions?", Lucas asked, turning his neck in her direction.

"I can't think of anything either", Shelia said, scratching her head.

"Well, as the campaign goes along, I know that both of you will have questions. Feel free to call my office or send me an email anytime. I'm going to head home now and y' all have a great evening", Clarence said, rising up.

"Thank you for stopping by Clarence and we appreciate it", Lucas said.

"Thank you, Clarence,", Shelia said.

"You're both welcome", Clarence said.

Clarence gets up from the sofa and Lucas and Shelia shake Clarence's hand. He leaves a short time later and a week later, Shelia is at home and it's the early afternoon. She's doing some housework when the phone rings and Shelia answers and it's her younger sister Janet.

"Hello Janet", Shelia said.

"Hello Shelia and how is my big sister doing? How's the family?", Janet asked.

"We're fine and I was doing some housework. How is my little sister doing?", Shelia asked.

"I'm okay. What do you have planned for the rest of the day Shelia?", Janet asked.

"I was going to finish this housework and then relax. Why do you ask? What's up?", Shelia asked.

"It's been quite a while since we've spent time with each other. I wanted to take you out to dinner today."

"You're right Janet, but this house needs some work. I've been putting it off for too long."

"Shelia, you take pride in keeping your house clean and I'm pretty sure that it's not that bad."

"I disagree Janet."

"I want us to check out Quincy's Soul Food Restaurant. I've heard that their food is pretty good. I would enjoy the experience more if you would come with me", Janet said.

"After a great family sales pitch like that, how can I refuse?", Shelia asked.

"Okay, what time did you want me to pick you up?", Janet asked.

"Five o' clock would be a good time."

"That works for me."

"I'll see you then Janet. Good-bye."

"Good-bye Shelia."

Four hours later, Shelia and Janet are sitting down in the restaurant. They're enjoying their meals and each other's company. While they're eating, Shelia raves about the food.

"Janet, this barbecue chicken and potato salad is great! I'm happy that you brought me here and I'll definitely come back to this restaurant", Shelia said.

"And I love their ribs too", Janet said.

"They're going to do some good business in Center City."

"I agree."

"I'm happy that we're hanging out and we need to do this more often."

"I agree and we will. Shelia, I have something that I need to tell you", Janet said.

"What is it?", Shelia asked.

"Shelia, I wanted to tell you this face-to-face instead of over the phone."

"Janet, you're making me nervous. What is it? What's wrong?"

Janet lets out a long, dreadful sigh. Then she pauses to put together the words that she wants to express and answers Shelia.

"Shelia, I went to my doctor for an examination and she discovered that I have Breast Cancer", Janet said.

Shelia's facial expression turns into shock and disbelief. She drops her fork and it bounces in various directions on her plate and she gives Janet a blank stare. Shelia is temporarily quiet and then gathers together her thoughts and then Shelia speaks to her.

"Maybe your doctor's diagnosis was wrong. Maybe you should get a second opinion", Shelia suggested.

"I already did and the result was the same. The reality is that I have Breast Cancer", Janet said.

"Well, maybe you should get a third opinion."

"I could, but I don't believe that the diagnosis will change."

"Janet, when I talked to you on the phone, why did you say that you were okay?"

"Because I thought that it would be easier to tell you in person. I also wanted us to enjoy each other and a great meal."

"Have you told our parents?", Shelia asked.

"I have and they were devastated, especially Mom", Janet said.

"How far has the cancer spread?"

"Well, the good news is that they discovered the cancer in its early stage. This significantly increases the odds for successful treatment."

"Thank God", Shelia said, letting out a sigh of relief.

"I'm thankful that I give myself a monthly breast self-exam. One morning, I examined my breasts and I felt a lump on my breast and noticed some redness. I was concerned and I made a doctors' appointment the same day", Janet said.

"I'm glad that you did."

"Me too."

"When do you start your treatments Janet?"

"Not right away Shelia. Next week I'm going to have surgery and then they'll begin my radiation treatments."

"I'll be praying for you."

"Thank you Shelia and I feel that the surgery will be successful. My doctor is optimistic."

"That's a good sign."

"Now, let's get off this negative talk. It's a beautiful day, and let's enjoy it", Janet said.

"You're right and don't hesitate to call if you need anything", Shelia said.

"I will and I love you Shelia."

"I love you too Janet."

An hour later, Shelia and Janet leave the restaurant. Fifteen minutes later, Janet drops Shelia off at home. When Shelia walks in, Lucas greets her cheerfully.

"Shelia, I saw the note that you left on the television. Did you and Janet have a good time? How is she?", Lucas asked.

"Well, we had a great time, but I'm concerned about her", Shelia said.

"Why? What's wrong?"

"Janet has Breast Cancer, but they caught it in the early stage."

"What did you say Shelia?", Lucas asked, in disbelief.

"Lucas, she was diagnosed with Breast Cancer", Shelia said.

"Wow! This is terrible news and I feel bad for Janet", Lucas said.

"Well, at least they caught it early and all things considered, she's in good spirits."

"I'll be praying for her."

"Me too. Her doctor is optimistic about her surgery and future treatments."

"When will they start treating her?"

"Next week Janet's going to have surgery and then she'll begin her treatments", Shelia said.

"Make sure that you stay in touch with her and tell her that we're here for her", Lucas said.

"I will and Janet's going to need a lot of support. My little sister is a tough lady and I believe that she will pull through this", Shelia said, confidently.

"With prayers and support, she can", Lucas said.

"I agree."

Nothing special happens the rest of the day and one month later, Lucas is sitting in his office at work. He's enjoying a Mc Donald's Big Mac Combo during the employees' lunch break when he hears someone knocking on his door. Lucas can see through his glass door that it's his plant manager Tommy Madison and his employees Joyce Haynes and Ken Bankart. He motions for them to enter his office and Tommy opens the door. They enter and Joyce is holding a piggy bank and Lucas is curious as to why she brought a piggy bank and asks her about it.

"Lucas, we love you and want you to be the Mayor of Butlerville. Some of us contributed money into this piggy bank to help support your campaign. We hope that this will help you get off to a good start", Joyce said, giving him the piggy bank.

"We're rooting for you Lucas", Ken said, pumping his fists.

"And there's a note in there", Joyce said.

"Thank you so much everyone and I promise that I will use your money wisely. I will do everything that I can to justify your faith in me", Lucas said, grateful.

"You should open your bank"", Tommy suggested.

"I'll do that right now."

Lucas opens it and can see a variety of different dollar bills and he picks up the note. He begins reading it and the note says, "LUCAS LIGHTFOOT, WE WISH YOU WELL IN YOUR MAYORAL CAMPAIGN AND YOU'RE THE BEST!" Lucas is visibly emotional and becomes choked up and tears begin squirting from his eyes. Joyce walks over to a table and tears off a piece of paper towel and hands it to Lucas. He thanks her and dries his eyes and Lucas gathers his thoughts and then addresses everyone.

"This is one of the nicest things that anyone has ever done for me. I'll never forget it and thank you everyone", Lucas said.

"You're welcome Lucas and be careful with the money. Make sure that you place it in a secure place", Tommy suggested.

"I'll deposit it into my bank account", Lucas said.

"Well Lucas, break time is almost over and we just wanted to do that for you", Joyce said.

"I really appreciate this and I'll be on the plant floor in about five minutes."

"Okay", Tommy said.

Lucas works the rest of his day in good spirits and an optimism that he hasn't felt in some time. Occasionally, he hums and sings his favorite songs and smiles more than usual. At the end of the work shift, Lucas wishes his employees a good evening and then heads home. Two months later, Lucas and Shelia are in Butlerville campaigning door to door and it's the late evening. The sun is beginning to go down and the sky is becoming dark. They approach one house and Lucas rings the residence's doorbell three times and then he takes two steps backward. A short time later, an elderly white lady comes to the door, but doesn't open it and asks whom it is. Lucas tells her that he's running for Mayor and asks her if she's made up her mind about whom she's going to vote for. The lady opens the door and she is horrified when she sees Lucas and Shelia and immediately slams the door. They're shocked at the lady's action, but then shake it off and go to other houses. At one of them, a middle-aged white man answers his door and Lucas introduces himself and Shelia.

"Hello sir. My name is Lucas Lightfoot and this is my wife, Shelia. I'm running for Mayor of Butlerville and have you made up your mind about whom you're going to vote for?", Lucas asked.

"I recognize you. You were the man that saved Mayor Lane's life at Mc Donald's", he said.

"Really? You were there?"

"I was and that was some quick thinking on your part. I'm sorry, I forgot to tell Ya'll my name and it's Myron, he said, extending his hand toward Lucas.

"Nice to meet you Myron", Lucas said, shaking his hand.

"Nice to meet you Shelia."

"Same here Myron", Shelia said, shaking his hand.

"To answer your earlier question, I have not made up my mind yet. I'm an independent voter."

"What do you think are the most pressing problems in Butlerville? If I'm elected, what would you like me to do to solve the problems?"

"Bring family supporting jobs to Butlerville and invest more money into our mental health facilities. We have also experienced an increase in crimes related to mental illnesses."

"Jobs are my number one priority and I will address Butlerville's mental illness problem."

"The high unemployment rate in Butlerville negatively affects our quality of life and creates depression."

"I agree. I will offer companies tax credits and other incentives to motivate them to relocate to Butlerville", Lucas said.

"I like that idea. I can imagine how tired and hungry that you and your wife must be from campaigning. My wife Candy just finished cooking dinner and we have chicken, meatloaf, and macaroni and cheese. Would y' all like a plate?", Myron asked.

"Oh no, we couldn't impose like that. We---

"It's not a problem. We always fix some extra food just in case we have visitors."

"We don't want y' all going through all that trouble", Shelia said.

"Y' all come in", Myron said, motioning toward the house.

"Okay. Thank you for your hospitality", Lucas said.

"You're welcome."

They walk into the house and Myron introduces them to Candy. She gives them a warm welcome and they escort Lucas and Shelia into the kitchen. They encourage them to load their plates and when Lucas and Shelia are finished, Myron and Candy ask them if they want to stay and eat their food. Lucas and Shelia politely decline and ask them if they have aluminum foil to cover their plates. Myron takes a roll of foil from the top of the refrigerator and hands it to Shelia. They tear off their pieces and cover their plates and thank

Myron and Candy for their generosity. A short time later, Lucas and Shelia decide to leave and as they're heading toward the front door, Myron asks Lucas how well his campaigning is going.

"I'm not sure Myron. Most people have been friendly to us, but I don't know if that will translate into votes", Lucas said.

"You're probably doing better than you think Lucas. Don't give up and continue working hard", Myron said.

"Thank you for your encouraging words."

"You're welcome and you've earned my vote Mr. Lightfoot. Good luck to you", Myron said, giving Lucas and Shelia a thumbs up.

"Thank you and I appreciate that", Lucas said, beaming.

Moments later, Lucas and Shelia leave and decide to end their campaigning for the day. A month later, it's the first week of November and it's election night at the Overton Dancehall. Lucas asks Clarence to update him on the election results.

"Lucas, right now, Nate Greenburg is ahead sixty percent to forty-percent. The good news is that the night is still young and only twenty percent of the votes have been counted. Hang in there Lucas", Clarence said, optimistically.

"Thank you for giving it to me straight", Lucas said, grimly.

"Dad, the election isn't over until the final vote is counted", Melvin said, patting Lucas on the shoulder.

"Lucas, you still have a chance. Don't throw in the towel", Shelia said.

"Dad, you've always told us to do our best and never give up", Chester said.

"Well, I guess a slim chance is better than no chance", Lucas remarked.

"Exactly and that's a good way of looking at this. Win or lose Lucas, our family is proud of what you've accomplished."

"Thank you Shelia."

"Me too Lucas. You've done very well, especially for someone that ran for public office for the first time", Clarence said.

"Thank you, Clarence. I couldn't have done this without the support of my family and you", Lucas said.

113

"Let's continue to monitor the progress of the election."

"Okay."

An hour later, Lucas' campaign team is gathered around a television and the updated election results run across the screen. Fox nine news show that Lucas is leading the Mayoral Race, with fifty-one percent of the vote, with ninety-five percent of the precincts reporting. Lucas is shocked and his family is delighted for him and they cross their fingers and remain hopeful that Lucas will win. Thirty minutes later, Clarence approaches Lucas with a cell phone in his hand. He indicates to Lucas that he has an important call that he should accept and Lucas asks Clarence whom it is. Clarence urges Lucas to talk to the person, while pointing the phone toward him. Reluctantly, Lucas takes the phone from Clarence and speaks to the caller.

"Hello", Lucas said.

"Hello Mayor-Elect Lightfoot. This is Nate Greenburg and I'm calling to concede defeat. Congratulations on your victory and you ran a great campaign", Nate said.

"Thank you, Mayor Greenburg!", Lucas said, shocked.

"You're welcome. Even though we're on opposite ends of the political spectrum, we both share a desire to improve the quality of life for Butlerville residents. Mayor-Elect Lightfoot, I'll help you in any way that I can, and don't hesitate to call me. I won't create any problems for you."

"I so appreciate that Mayor Greenburg and I will definitely keep that in mind!"

"Well, congratulations again and good-bye."

"Good-bye."

Lucas hangs up and has a Kool-Aid smile on his face. He walks up to a podium and signals for everyone's attention. They become quiet and direct their attention toward him and moments later, Lucas makes the announcement to everyone.

"My family, friends, and supporters, I just got off the phone with Interim Mayor Nate Greenburg. He just called and congratulated me on being elected the Mayor of Butlerville! I want to thank everyone for their hard work, prayers, support, and believing in Lucas Lightfoot!", Lucas said.

His crowd of supporters roar their approval with almost deafening noise. Some of them yell out, "Mayor Lightfoot! Mayor Lightfoot!" for minutes. Lucas moves his hands up and down, indicating to them that he wants to continue speaking. Everyone calms down and become quiet and then Lucas resumes speaking.

"I promise the citizens of Butlerville that I'll wake up every morning and serve you to the best of my ability. I will always look out for your best interests even if opposing forces don't want me to. Honor and Integrity will always be the hallmarks of the Lightfoot Administration!"

"Mayor Lightfoot is the man!", one man yelled out.

"We love you Mayor Lightfoot!" a woman yelled out.

"I want to thank my great wife Shelia and my sons Chester and Melvin for their love and support. They put in many miles walking door to door with me. They encouraged me, especially when things got tough and I thought about quitting. I want to thank my great campaign manager Clarence Backman and his staff of volunteers. Clarence was patient with me and did a great job educating me about politics. This would not be a reality without them."

"Lucas! Lucas!", his supporters shouted.

"Thank you everyone once again for your support. Have a great night and enjoy the celebration and then drive home safely!", Lucas warned.

Lucas leaves the podium and shakes the hands of his supporters and they congratulate him on his victory. Others take pictures of and him and his family, while some other supporters and residents ask for his autograph. Thirty minutes later, Lucas notices that besides the local news media, national media outlets are now in the Overton Dancehall. CNN reporter Spencer Mason approaches Lucas and begins to interview him about his Mayoral Victory.

"Mayor-Elect Lightfoot, how does it feel to become the first African-American Mayor of Butlerville?", Spencer asked.

"I don't believe that the citizens of Butlerville care about that. They expect me to solve their problems and if I don't, they're going to elect someone else", Lucas said.

"Why do you think that the residents of Butlerville elected you?"

"I listened to their concerns and I believe they wanted a fresh voice. I believe that they were tired of the same old politics."

"What are you going to do after you're sworn in as Mayor?"

"Too many residents of Butlerville are financially struggling to make ends meet. I'm going to sit down and brainstorm ideas with our city council members and our chamber of commerce. We're going to work together and come up with a new economic development plan for Butlerville."

News reporters from various media outlets continue interviewing Lucas for another half an hour. When they're finished, Lucas begins to party and celebrate with his family and supporters. They celebrate until a little past midnight before everyone begins leaving. Lucas and his family are the last ones to leave and they cheer and sing various celebration songs on their way home. The following day, Lucas is at work and the employee lunch break has just begun. Lucas begins walking toward his office when Joyce Haynes and Ken Bankart spot Lucas and walk over to him. They ask him to come into the break room and his facial expression turns into a frown, but he agrees to go with them. Moments later, they walk in and Lucas sees that the break room is crowded with some well-dressed men and women. They're obviously influential people and Lucas scans the room and some of his employees are smiling approvingly at him. Others are cheering and pumping their fists into the air. Still others are yelling out his name and Lucas is obviously moved. Minutes later, everyone gets up and gives Lucas a round of applause and they clap their hands furiously with joy. Lucas thanks everyone for their support and he enjoys the moment. A short time later, Tommy Madison instructs everyone to sit down and be quiet because he has an important announcement. They follow his instructions and then Tommy begins speaking to the group.

"Thank you everyone for giving our great supervisor Lucas Lightfoot such a great reception. We're so proud of him becoming Mayor of Butlerville. Lucas, I'm personally proud of you, not only as your boss, but also as a friend", Tommy said, looking at Lucas.

"Thank you, Tommy, and everyone. I'll never forget this", Lucas said, humbled.

"Lucas, our corporate president, Rudy Wagner is here. He wants to present you with some things to honor your achievement. Rudy, the room is yours," Tommy said, pointing toward him.

"Thank you, Tommy. Lucas, we wish you well in your job as Mayor. We want to help you get started off on the right foot and we want to present you with some gifts. We want to give you an engraved name plate, a suit and a tie, and dress shoes. And we want to give you this five-hundred-dollar gift card from our friends at Walmart", Rudy said.

Rudy walks over to Lucas and gives him the items and they exchange firm handshakes. Lucas thanks Rudy and everyone applauds and a short time later, Lucas speaks to everyone.

"Thank you for your love and support and believing in me, even when I had doubts. Thank you for raising money for my campaign and spreading the message of what I stand for. Have a great rest of the day!"

Lucas then turns to Tommy and Rudy and chats with them and the rest of the corporate staff for ten minutes. When Lucas finishes talking with them, he walks toward his supervisor's office to eat his lunch. The rest of the work day goes smoothly and three and a half hours later, Lucas' shift has ended and he's in great spirits. On his way home, he decides to buy Shelia a bouquet of red roses and a Hallmark greeting card. When Lucas enters Center City, he stops at Connie's Flowers and Garden and when he walks in, he's greeted by a friendly, beautiful young black woman. She asks Lucas if he needs help or suggestions and he tells her that he wants to browse and she respects his wish. He studies various roses and flowers and he decides to buy Shelia a dozen red roses. He then sorts through a variety of greeting cards before finally settling on one and Lucas walks toward the counter and pays for the items. He walks out and he arrives home ten minutes later. Before he gets out of the car, he thinks about what message that he wants to place inside of Shelia's greeting card. After several minutes of deep thought, he pulls an ink pen out of his pants pocket and writes inside the card. When Lucas is finished, he gets out of the car and moments later, he enters their home. Shelia hears him coming and gets up from the living room sofa to greet him. Lucas sees her coming and quickly puts the roses and card behind him and when Shelia greets him, she frowns and wonders why his hands are behind his back. Shelia asks Lucas why and he smiles and gives her the roses and greeting card. Shelia is pleasantly surprised and she gives Lucas numerous kisses and hugs. He encourages her to read the greeting card and Shelia asks Lucas to hold the roses while she reads it. Shelia reads it slowly and toward the end of the message, a line written by Lucas particularly warms her heart, it says, "I HAVE THE BEST WIFE THAT A MAN COULD HAVE AND MY LIFE HAS AND CONTINUES TO BE RICHER BECAUSE OF YOU", LOVE FOREVER, LUCAS, and a heart with a smiley face is next to the message. Shelia is temporarily silent and then tears begin rolling down her cheeks and she thanks Lucas for his loving gesture. Lucas tells her that it was no problem and then grabs a couple of Kleenex out of a box sitting on the television and dries her face. Three days later, Lucas and Shelia are at home enjoying a pleasant afternoon and watching television in their living room. The phone rings and Lucas rises up from the sofa and the number of the Center City Town Hall is appearing on the Caller ID. Lucas frowns and has some reluctance about answering it, but a soft, sub conscience voice urges him to answer it and Lucas picks it up.

"Hello", Lucas said.

"Hello. May I speak with Mayor-Elect Lightfoot? This is Mayor Johnson B. Sanders of Center City", he said.

"Wow! Mayor Sanders, this is Lucas Lightfoot and this is such a pleasant surprise! How are you?", Lucas asked.

"I'm fine. I wanted to call and congratulate you on your historic election victory", Mayor Sanders said.

"Thank you, Mayor Sanders,", Lucas said.

"Mayor-Elect Lightfoot, you've made Center City proud! We want to honor you this coming Tuesday at the Center City Town Hall and we would like to proclaim it "Lucas Lightfoot Day." We want to give you the key to the city."

"Wow, Mayor Sanders! I'm so honored and I don't know if I'm worthy of such an honor. I'm just a working man that tries to live the right way and provide the best life that I can for my family."

"Lucas, you're being too modest and you've achieved something extraordinary."

"I'm at a loss for words", Lucas said.

"Lucas, would you be interested in coming to the Town Hall? Would it be convenient for you and your family?", Mayor Sanders asked.

"My family would be thrilled."

"Would one o' clock be a good time?"

"One o' clock would be a great time."

"Wonderful. Mayor-Elect Lightfoot, we look forward to seeing you and your family. Good-bye and have a great day", Mayor Sanders said.

"Thank you Mayor Sanders and we'll definitely be there. Good-bye and you have a great day as well", Lucas said.

Lucas hangs up has a huge smile on his face and Shelia asks him why Mayor Sanders called.

"Shelia, you're not going to believe this! Mayor Sanders wants to present me with the key to Center City on Tuesday!', Lucas said, thrilled.

"That's great Lucas and I'm so happy for you!", Shelia said, excited.

"The Mayor and I scheduled the ceremony for one o' clock on Tuesday. It's going to be great to have my family there to share this honor with me."

"You deserve this so much Lucas."

"It feels like I'm daydreaming", Lucas said.

"This is really happening Lucas", Shelia assured him.

"I can't believe that Center City is honoring me like this! America is a great country!"

"Now I have to go shopping for a special outfit."

"Shelia, you already have a lot of great outfits to wear. You're a beautiful, sexy woman and going shopping isn't necessary."

"Thank you for the compliment, Lucas, but it's necessary. It's not every day that a lady's husband is honored with a key to the city. I want to look my best for you."

"Shelia, I don't know what I would do without you. You've been such a great wife and partner to me and you've always had my back. Chester and Melvin are blessed to have a great mother like you. Shelia, I love you so much and I feel like the most blessed man in the world."

"Aw Lucas. I---

Shelia is overcome with emotion and tears begin rolling down her cheeks. She reaches over and passionately kisses and hugs Lucas tightly and tells him that she loves him. He returns the messages and then wipes away her tears with loving eyes. Minutes later, they cuddle and resume watching television and nothing special happens the rest of the day. Three days later, it's Tuesday afternoon, and Lucas, his family, and Shelia's family walk into the Center City Town Hall. Local reporters are also there to cover the ceremony and Lucas and everyone meet and shake the hands of Mayor Sanders, his Chief of Staff Cheryl Bailey, and the Center City Council Members. A short time later, Lucas and his family and Shelia's parents, Wendy and Arthur Lawson sit down in their designated seats. Everyone patiently waits for Mayor Sanders to enter the room and minutes later, Mayor Sanders enters the room. He smiles and waves to everyone as he approaches his podium. He thanks everyone for showing up and then begins his remarks.

"Good afternoon, everyone. I am honored to be here and give special recognition to Mayor-Elect Lucas Lightfoot of Butlerville.

He's a son of Center City and he's made us proud. Mayor-Elect Lightfoot is an inspiration to not only black people, but to Americans of all races."

Mayor Sanders clears his throat and drinks a couple of sips of water and then resumes speaking.

"Mayor Lightfoot is a good role model and our young people can look at him and say to themselves, "I can grow up and be Mayor too." As Mayor of Center City, I proclaim this to be Lucas Lightfoot Day on this date of November eleventh, two thousand and eighteen. And on behalf of myself, Chief of Staff, City Council members, and residents of Center City, I give you the key to Center City. Congratulations."

Everyone claps and applauds Lucas as he gets up and walks toward the podium. When he arrives there, Lucas greets the Mayor and they exchange firm hand shakes, along with Chief of Staff Cheryl Bailey. Moments later, Lucas addresses the audience.

"Mayor Sanders, Chief of Staff Bailey, and City Council members, thank you for this honor. This is such a blessing and no one receives this honor without help. I've had the support of a great family, my wife Shelia and our two sons, and my parents. Shelia was right by my side when I was door-to-door campaigning and encouraged me to continue, even when I wanted to quit. Chester and Melvin reminded me that we always taught them the importance of hard work. They hung in there with me, even when I got on their nerves", Lucas said, laughing.

Shelia and the other family members laugh along with some audience members. Moments later, they calm down and Lucas resumes his speech.

"My loving parents taught me to always give my best effort. They taught me the importance of treating people the right way and keeping your word. When you promise someone that you're going to do something, you should follow through, even if it's not convenient. My parents are good and honorable people and I'm blessed to have them as parents. Thank you, Mom and Dad,", Lucas said, looking directly at them.

Everyone cheers and Lucas' parents are visibly touched by his praise. His mother has tears squirting out of her eyes and she gives Lucas a thumbs up and he gives her one in return. His father looks at his mother and tells her, "That's our son!" and pumps a fist into the air and Lucas acknowledges him. A short time later, the audience becomes silent and Lucas scans the room and then resumes speaking.

"My campaign manager, Clarence Wickman is a gracious and kind man. I couldn't have had a better campaign manager. And my volunteers did an amazing job and I thank them for their selfless time that they spent helping me get elected. I will be forever grateful to them. Thank you everyone for coming out to support me and have a great rest of the day", Lucas said, waving to the crowd.

The audience members rise up out of their chairs and they cheer and applaud Lucas. While everyone is cheering, Mayor Sanders shakes Lucas' hand and then gives him a proclamation plaque. Lucas holds the plaque and shows it off by moving it in various directions with pride. When he's finished, the mayor presents Lucas with a beautiful red case that contains the key to the city. Lucas leaves the podium to rejoin his family and they hug and embrace him in what seems like an eternity. When they're finished, Shelia speaks to him.

"Lucas, I don't think that I've been more proud of you!", Shelia said.

"Thank you Shelia", Lucas said.

"Dad, you're the best!", Chester said, excited.

"We have the world's best father!", Melvin said, proudly.

"Sons, I think that you're both over doing the compliments, but I appreciate them."

"I've been bragging to my college friends about you Dad. I think that some of them are jealous."

"I've been bragging too Dad. Some of my college professors asked me about you", Chester said.

"It feels great to say that our father has made Black History!", Melvin said, proudly.

"Chester and Melvin, both of you have been great sons. It's been a privilege for your Mother and I to have raised y' all.

"We're blessed to have you and Mom."

"Lucas, I'm so proud of you son", Aaron said.

"Thank you Dad", Lucas said.

"You've turned out to be a damn good man and you've honored the Lightfoot name forever."

"Dad, you and Mom taught me values and morals that I try to live up to daily. I know that I'm a flawed man and I have my hang ups, because I'm human. But I never want my family to feel that I've let them down and the thought of something like that scares me."

"Lucas, the only perfect person died on the cross for us. No one should ever expect perfection and all we should do is give our best effort. When we make mistakes, we should try and learn from them and become a better person."

"I try to do that Dad. I---

"Lucas, words can't even begin to describe how proud I am of you! They gave you the key to Center City!", Denise said.

"Thank you Mom and I still can't believe it!", Lucas said.

"This is a great day in the history of our family."

"You're right Mom."

"Lucas, we're all going to treat you to lunch and we're going to Applebee's! I hope that your appetite is ready!", Shelia said.

"Well, I am a little hungry", Lucas said, laughing.

"Good. You're going to have a full belly", Shelia said, smiling.

Several minutes later, they leave the town hall and head to Applebee's for lunch. They celebrate Lucas' accomplishments and enjoy each other's company for a couple of hours before leaving. Later that night, Lucas and Shelia are in their bedroom and Lucas has finished taking a shower. He dries himself off and puts on his red robe, t-shirt, and underwear and then comes out of the bathroom. He sees Shelia laying on their bed and she seductively stares at him. She is wearing a black bra and thong and Shelia begins rubbing her horny pussy and then closes her eyes and begins moaning. Moments later, she opens her eyes and speaks to Lucas.

"Hello Mayor Lightfoot. Do you like what you see?", Shelia asked.

"I sure do Mrs. Lightfoot", Lucas said.

"Good. Why don't you come over here and get a better look?", Shelia asked.

"You don't have to tell me twice!", Lucas said.

Lucas' eyes light up and he removes his clothes and leaves them in the middle of the floor. He joins her in the bed and Shelia spreads her legs and Lucas hovers over her. He leans forward and they begin kissing passionately for a couple of minutes and then Shelia interrupts the kissing. She tells Lucas that she wants to remove her bra and he gets up off her temporarily. Shelia rises up and removes it and throws it to the opposite side of the bed and then Lucas begins massaging her chest in various directions. Shelia closes her eyes again and moans while enjoying Lucas' magical hands and a short time later, Lucas leans forward and begins licking and sucking her rock-hard nipples. Shelia's body makes a sudden jerking motion and she moans delightfully and encourages him to continue. Lucas honors Shelia's request and this continues for five minutes. Lucas then begins working his way down Shelia's body, rubbing and kissing it and occasionally using some precise tongue action. Eventually, he arrives at Shelia's smoking hot pussy and carefully removes her thong and throws it to the side. Moments later, he begins licking her clit with precision and her body begins to quiver and she yells out his name, "Lucas! Lucas!" This motivates Lucas to do even more and he gently inserts a finger into her volcanic pussy. He twists and turns his finger from right to left, and vice versa. Minutes later, a waterfall of pussy juices come out of her and spread all over Lucas' fingers. After her pussy faucet stops, Shelia catches her breath and lets out a long, joyful sigh and then crawls toward Lucas' dick. She holds it with both hands and gently massages his pole up and down and then Shelia begins sucking his hot dog with no hands. Lucas moans approvingly and minutes later, Lucas yells out, "Shelia, this feels so good!" She stops temporarily and looks up at Lucas and tells him, "I'm glad that you love it, Lucas!" and then resumes sucking his dick. She deep throats his hot dog and Lucas' body becomes temporarily paralyzed and once again Lucas moans with delight. Several minutes later, Lucas tells Shelia that he wants them to switch positions and he wants her in the missionary position and she cooperates. Lucas inserts his steel pole into her flaming hot pussy and Shelia reaches her arms and hands toward Lucas. She puts her hands on his shoulders and they lovingly smile and look deeply into each other's eyes. Lucas places his hands flat on the bed and Shelia lifts her legs and he begins pumping his dick into her moist pussy. Lucas smoothly moves his body forward and backward and intensely fucks her pussy cave. This continues for twenty minutes and then Lucas removes his dick and indicates to Shelia that he wants to tit fuck her. Shelia is agreeable and Lucas inserts his brick hard dick in between her huge tits and he puts them together and they smother his dick. Lucas moves his pole up and down like a new elevator and occasionally kisses and sucks her nipples. Minutes later, Lucas squirts out a huge load of milky white cream and splatters it all over Shelia's huge melons while letting out a sigh of joyous relief. Moments later, Lucas and Shelia are laying side-by-side and reflecting on their great sexual adventure. When they're finished, they both get up and wash themselves up. When they're done, Lucas and Shelia watch some television before eventually falling asleep. A week later, Lucas is at work and he's in Tommy's office upstairs and they're discussing Lucas' future.

"Lucas, we know that it's going to be difficult for you to perform your job here and also prepare for your job as Mayor", Tommy said.

"It's funny that you should say that because I was wondering how I was going to balance the two", Lucas said.

"I've been talking to our corporate people about your situation."

"You have?"

"Yes, I have and I worked out a situation that I think you will like."

"What is it?"

"Well, you're going to sworn in as Mayor of Butlerville in January. I know that putting together your administration is going to take up a lot of your time", Tommy said.

"You're right", Lucas said.

"Our corporate executives want you to succeed and we came up with a solution for you. Of course, it's up to you whether you want to advantage of it."

"What's the solution?"

"B. Mitchell has offered to pay you your regular salary until you're sworn in as Mayor", Tommy said.

"I don't understand Tommy. I'm going to be working here, so I'm supposed to be earning my regular salary", Lucas reasoned.

"You don't have to work here anymore if you don't want to Lucas. B. Mitchell is saying that you can quit and they'll still pay you your regular salary until you're sworn in as Mayor", Tommy said.

"Tommy, are you kidding? Did I hear you right?"

"I'm not joking Lucas. Next week can be your last employment week if you want it to be", Tommy said.

"I'm just curious; whom would take over my position?", Lucas asked.

"I would take over your position until we hired someone permanent."

"Wow! Thank you Tommy and you've been so generous. I'm at a loss for words."

"You're welcome Lucas. So are you going to keep working here or are you going to quit next week?", Tommy asked.

"Naturally I'm going to quit next week", Lucas said, smiling.

"Good. I'll let our corporate executives know so that it'll become official."

"Thank you so much Tommy!"

"You're welcome Lucas."

They chat for several more minutes and then Lucas tells Tommy that he has to get back to work. They both rise up from their chairs and exchange firm handshakes and then Lucas leaves. The rest of the day is uneventful and a week later, it's Thanksgiving Day. Lucas and his family are sitting around the kitchen table and he's leading them in a prayer of thanks. When he's finished, they all say "Amen!" and Lucas addresses the family.

"This is a beautiful thing to have our family here and everyone is doing well. We all have our health, strength, and each other", Lucas said, thankful.

"You're right Lucas and this is such a blessing", Shelia said.

"Our family has a lot to be thankful for."

"We sure do."

"Sons, how have y' all been coming along in College?", Lucas asked, looking in their direction.

"Dad, it took some time for me to adjust to the College Lifestyle, but I think that I've pretty much figured it out. I've never been a morning person and that was one of my biggest adjustments. Those eight a.m. classes were brutal, but I knocked them out and I'm used to them now", Chester said.

"I can relate to that Chester because there are some mornings when I hate turning the bed loose. I have to get ready for work, whether I want to or not. But, part of life is forcing yourself to do things when you don't want to", Lucas said.

"And I had trouble balancing my school work and playing basketball. But, Coach Davenport helped me get through it and my college professors and friends also helped me."

"Life is easier when people encourage and support you."

"It sure is."

"And I know that there are a lot of attractive young ladies on your campus. There's nothing wrong with having a steady girlfriend, as long as you don't let the relationship negatively affect your school work", Lucas warned.

"I hear what you're saying Dad, but I've been so busy that it's difficult to have a girlfriend", Chester said.

"I can imagine."

"Chester, how are your grades?", Shelia asked.

"I have a B average", Chester said.

"That's good and I want you to challenge yourself and try for an A average. We know that you can do it."

"I'll try Mom and I'll work harder in the classroom."

"Alright."

"Mom, this chicken and dressing is really good", Chester said.

"Thank you, Chester, and help yourself to some more. Melvin, how are you coming along in college", Shelia asked.

"I'm doing pretty well and I have a three-point five grade point average. I made the right decision to attend Southern Ilinois University and the people are so friendly and helpful", Melvin said.

"That's great."

"And I also made the right decision by majoring in Education and I love it! One of my professors told me that he believes that I could become a superstar educator. That made me feel good and there's a shortage of educators in the United States. He told me that there is a low number of black men teaching in schools."

"He's right about that. Throughout my school years, I can only remember about two, maybe three black men that were teaching my classes", Lucas said, shaking his head.

"That's a sad and pitiful reality", Melvin said.

"It is, but you can help change that, Melvin. One day, with hard work, you could become the United States Secretary of Education. You could follow in the footsteps of Rod Paige and become the second African-American to hold that position."

"I never thought about that."

"You can do something like that Melvin and why shouldn't it be you?", Shelia asked.

"Maybe I could do something like that", Melvin said.

"Of course, you can do something like that. You're our son", Lucas said, proudly.

"Dad, you did a great job of hooking up this turkey and cranberry sauce. I've been savoring every bite!"

"Thank you Melvin. Don't hesitate to get some more because we have plenty", Lucas said, beaming.

"This is a great Thanksgiving", Shelia said.

"It sure is", Lucas agreed.

They continue eating and enjoying each other's company. When they're finished, their stomachs are full and everyone washes their dishes. As the day goes on, relatives and friends come over and spend time with them. Later that night, the family sits in the living room and watch the Chicago Bears defeat the Detroit Lions, twenty-four to seventeen. After the game is over, Lucas and his family have a conversation and reflect on the beauty of the day and share some of their hopes and dreams. A couple of hours later, everyone retires to their bedrooms for the night. Two weeks later, Shelia is at home alone on her day off and she's lying-in bed and watching her favorite soap opera, The Young and the Restless. During a commercial break, the phone rings and Shelia rolls over toward a nearby night stand and looks to see whom it is. She sees the number of her younger sister Janet and she picks up the phone. Shelia clicks on the phone signal and speaks.

"Hello Janet and how is my great little sister?", Shelia asked.

"I'm fine Shelia and how is my great big sister? How is your family?", Janet asked.

"Everyone is fine", Shelia said.

"Good", Janet said.

"How is your health, Janet? Have you been eating healthy and drinking plenty of liquids?"

"Yes Shelia, I have been staying on top of my health. I thank you for your concern."

"No problem and I just want you to take care of yourself."

"I appreciate that Shelia and I called to share some great news with you."

"What is it, Janet?", Shelia asked.

"My doctor examined me a couple of days ago. My breast cancer has not come back or spread and my treatments have gone well! My health is improving and God is great!", Janet said.

"That's wonderful news!", Shelia said, excitedly.

"I've been doing a lot of praying and God answered my prayers!"

"Lucas and I have been praying for you!"

"Shelia, I have to admit that I've been more worried than I've been letting on."

"Well, you never fooled me Janet because I could sense your worrying."

"I've been scared and crossing my fingers. I'm going to continue praying", Janet said.

"And we'll be doing that right along with you", Shelia assured her.

"Thank you Shelia and I appreciate that."

"Just promise me that you'll continue to take care of yourself Janet."

"I'll definitely do that."

"That's what I want to hear."

"Shelia, I'm going to get off the phone now. I'm going to put some lunch into my tummy", Janet said, rubbing her stomach.

"Okay, you fill yourself up and thank you for sharing the great news", Shelia said.

"I'll talk to you later Shelia and I love you", Janet said.

"I love you too Janet", Shelia said.

"Good-bye."

"Bye."

Shelia hangs up and resumes watching The Young and the Restless and the rest of the day is uneventful. Two months later, it's a cold February morning in Butlerville and Lucas and his family are surrounded by former Mayor Lance Greenburg and the Butlerville City Council. Some residents of Butlerville and civic leaders are also joining them and they're standing by Robert E. Lee Boulevard. Some Butlerville City Workers are taking down the street and Confederate flag sign down. The workers replace the boulevard sign with President Barack Obama Boulevard and the Confederate flag sign is replaced with a United States flag. The workers put up a sign below the United States flag that says, "ALL GOOD AMERICANS ARE WELCOME IN BUTLERVILLE." When they're finished, everyone applauds, cheers, and claps their hands with pride and joy. They salute and thank the workers and Lucas and Shelia embrace and kiss each other. Chester and Melvin join them in a group hug and a short time later, Lance Greenburg and the city council members congratulate Lucas. He graciously accepts their gesture and they exchange firm handshakes and some of them pat Lucas on the back. Suddenly, some of the residents begin singing the Star-Spangled Banner and Lucas and his family join them and cover their chests with a hand. When they're finished, everyone celebrates and some of them give each other high fives. Others have tears rolling down their cheeks and still others are pumping their fists into the air. As the celebration winds down, people gradually leave and eventually, Lucas and his family are left. They bask in the glow of his achievement for several minutes and then Lucas speaks to his family.

"This is a great day for Butlerville and this is the beginning of a new era. This is the beginning of a city that works together and sees each other as Americans. It doesn't matter what race, gender, or sexual orientation you are", Lucas said, looking up at the new street sign.

"That's well stated Lucas", Shelia said, hugging him.

"Dad, you're a first-class father and we're so proud of you", Chester said.

"Me too Dad, and you're our hero", Melvin said.

"Thank you family", Lucas said.

Lucas is touched by their loving words and he can feel his eyes welling up with tears. Shelia opens up her purse and pulls out a couple of Kleenex and wipes the tears from his face. Shelia then plants kisses on his lips and she tells Lucas that she loves him and he tells her the same. Moments later, Lucas composes himself and gathers his thoughts and resumes speaking.

"Family, in my wildest dreams, I never thought that I would become an elected official. I especially never thought that I would be the mayor of a city", Lucas said.

"You're the Mayor of Butlerville", Shelia said.

"You're right Shelia and this reality is starting to hit me. I hope that I can serve the residents of Butlerville well. I---"

"Stop doubting yourself because you're going to do a great job Lucas", Shelia said, confidently.

"Dad, we're in your corner. We're going to help you succeed in any way that we can", Chester said.

"We have your back one hundred percent Dad", Melvin said.

"Family, I appreciate your support."

"Lucas, I know that Mayor Lane would be so proud of you", Shelia said.

"I wish that he was here", Lucas said.

"He might not be here physically, but I'm pretty sure that he's here in spirit. I can just imagine him smiling down on you."

"I hope that he is. Well family, are y' all hungry?", Lucas asked.

"I am", Shelia said, rubbing her stomach.

"What kind of food do you have a craving for?" I have a taste for some chicken, especially some Kentucky Fried Chicken."

"That sounds good to me. Sons, are y' all hungry?", Lucas asked.

"I am Dad. Chowing down some chicken is fine with me along with some coleslaw", Chester said.

"I'm okay with chicken too", Melvin said.

"Well, there's a KFC a couple of blocks from here. Let's head over there", Lucas said.

"And I'm pretty sure that they have some chicken specials", Shelia said.

"Me too."

Before they leave, Lucas and his family look up at the new street sign and then they get into Lucas' car. Moments later, he drives off.

Made in the USA
Monee, IL
01 April 2023

31020158R00083